PALIMPSEST

CAITLIN MARCEAU

Palimpsest

ISBN (paperback): 978-1-9196387-2-0

ISBN (e-book): 978-1-9196387-3-7

Cover illustration © LUMEZIA.com via. Shutterstock

Book formatting and cover design by Claire Saag

For Papa,

You shared stories with me growing up.

Now it's my turn to share them with you.

CONTENTS

FOREWORD

I'm beginning to think Caitlin Marceau has lost her writing rule book. No really, there are rule books, even Stephen King has written one. That's not to say she uses commas incorrectly, far from it. No it is because Caitlin Marceau, when tasked with creating a horror story, will do it however she damn well pleases. And it seems time and time again that her way is the right way.

I remember the first time I read a Marceau story. It opened on a protagonist lazily lying on the couch and quite simply *never moving from that spot*; frozen. A story is meant to take us places, or at least bring events to us and yet Caitlin decided to write a story that not only didn't go anywhere physically but *made that the story itself*. It's almost unfair to ignore all the conventions of writing and create something so brilliant and challenging. When you yourself read 'Stuck' in this collection, you'll see exactly what I mean.

Of course from this story alone I became an instant Marceau fan so when I personally commissioned Caitlin to write a ghost story, it was simply that: a ghost story. 'Something spooky, Caitlin, and please set it in your home country'. So naturally, Caitlin weaved an asthmatic protagonist into her heartbreaking tale, pulling the reader deeper into empathy and fear resulting in a tale that quite literally leaves the reader short of breath for layered reasons. I'm pleased to inform you, fellow reader, that you will also read this story in these very pages.

The more stories I read of Caitlin's, the more I realised this author was going by her own rules. 'Mr Perfect' was a story that pulled few punches but not in a gratuitous way (which frankly is too easily done in horror) but in ways that felt deeply sinister and necessary—'Mr Perfect' left me with a sense of unease, the sign of true horror story.

It seems nothing is truly off limits to Caitlin, whether an oddly prescient tale of a virus or tales of body horror and supernatural things—she not only dips her toes into such waters but dives deeply and resurfaces after a little too long under the surface.

Caitlin is truly one of the most exciting writers working today, master of many things and doing it entirely her own way.

Yes, there's a writing rule book somewhere in Caitlin's home, I'm sure of it. Under the couch, perhaps, gathering dust.

Pray she never finds it.

Mark Nixon

Editor, *Shadows at the Door: The Podcast*

County Durham, 2022

Run

Originally published in Shadows at the Door: An Anthology,

November 2016.

1968

Matthew stares at the clock over the blackboard and tries not to panic as the minute hand slowly makes its way to three in the afternoon. The classroom is bristling with excitement, students eager to leave school and go play with their friends, but for him it's another feeling entirely that fills his body and makes him sweat.

Fear.

Not that he'd ever admit it to anyone—a guy's got his pride—but the end of the school day always fills him with dread, and knowing that it's getting closer sends a chill down his spine and makes his hair stand on end. It normally wouldn't be so bad, but his last class of the day on Wednesdays is history, and he can feel two familiar sets of eyes watching him from the back of the room as the teacher drones on about this week's quiz.

Hoping that the teacher doesn't notice—she caught him last week and made him stay late to clap erasers—Matthew slowly begins to put his things in his school bag. He leaves his Hilroy copybook and nub of a pencil in full view, but sneaks his blue Bic pen and wooden ruler into the rectangular leather bag. He's in the middle of stuffing his thick brown-paper-wrapped history book and his duotang into the bag when the bell rings. It's loud, too loud, and it continues to ring in his head and make his teeth hurt even after it's stopped.

Not caring what gets crumpled, he stuffs the rest of his things in the backpack, buckles it shut, and runs for the door as fast as his legs can take him. He can feel the two boys not far behind him as he shoves his way down the halls and through the front door of Canon O'Meara Elementary School. He runs toward the small iron-wrought fence, grabs onto one of the pointed bars—careful not to impale himself like a boy had the year prior—and hoists himself over it. He lands shakily on the pavement and runs down Center Street. He can hear the two boys gaining on him, and doesn't need to check behind him to confirm what he already knows: they're going to catch him. He isn't fast enough.

He keeps running, desperately pushing forward even as he feels a hand wrap around the collar of his shirt. Pulling hard, the boy clothes-lines Matthew with his own shirt and lets out an obnoxious laugh as Matthew falls to the ground in front of Saint Gabriel's parish.

"Hey Mattie, where you going in such a rush?" asks Paul, the bigger of the two boys. His face is so fat it looks swollen, and his dark eyes stare at Matthew from behind disheveled brown hair. His blue plaid shirt is tucked into beige slacks, his brown belt pulled so tight at his waist that the leather looks to be cutting him in two.

Matthew looks up at him, coughing and rubbing his sore throat with his hand. When he doesn't answer, the boy kicks him hard in the ribs.

"Sorry, what was that?"

Matthew wants to answer, wants to curse him out, but his lungs are burning from running and he's starting to feel short of breath. He coughs louder this time, his chest impossibly tight. He takes his backpack off and pulls at the leather buckles, fumbling with the leather as the two boys laugh at his clumsiness. David, the smaller of the two bullies, moves to pull the bag out of Matthew's hand. Matthew reflexively punches him in the arm.

"Ow!" the boy yells, mostly out of surprise.

Matthew finally works the bag open and dumps the contents out on the asphalt. He rummages through the mess, panic slowly setting in as it gets harder to breathe, until he finally locates the Beclomethasone inhaler. He shakes the brown plastic tube, removes the mouth cap, and presses down on the metal aerosol canister as he inhales as deeply as his lungs will allow. A wave of relief washes over him as he tastes the bitter medicine and feels his lungs open, his breathing returning to normal.

He looks up to see a pair of hands grab his collar, and he doesn't fight back as Paul drags him to his feet, invading his personal space. The large boy reeks of sweat and his breath smells like the old bologna he had for lunch, and it takes all of Matthew's self-control not to shudder in disgust.

"You hit my friend," he says, pulling Matthew closer and enveloping him in the stench. "Big mistake. Didn't think you even knew how to make a fist, loser. Let me give you some pointers for next time."

Paul lets go of Matthew with one hand, holding him firm with the other. He draws his arm back, balling his meaty fingers into a fist, and smiles wide as Matthew tries not to flinch.

"Is there a problem here?"

Matthew sighs with relief as he spots Father John's annoyed expression from the steps of the old grey church. His thinning hair is brushed back and his black robes are spotless as always. His arms are crossed in front of his chest, and by the looks of things he hasn't come outside of his own good will. Behind him is a small boy with dirty blonde hair framing his thin, pointed face and big ears that stick out awkwardly from his head. His hand-me-down clothes are clearly two sizes too big. The boy wrings his hands, shrinking away from the boys on the road as though he's hoping no one will notice him standing there.

"No," David mutters, as Paul lets go of Matthew and takes a step back.

"Good. I'll see you boys on Sunday?"

"Yes, Father John," they all say in unison.

The priest waits by the door for the two larger boys to leave, grumbling to no one in particular when Paul makes a show of walking over Matthew's school things. He waits a moment longer, a scowl still fixed firmly on his face, before turning to head back inside the parish.

"Thank you," the small boy says in a soft voice as the priest passes, eyes fixed on the ground.

Father John nods, opens the heavy wooden door to the church, and closes it behind him. Once the older man is out of sight, the kid races down the steps and across the yard to his friend.

"Y'okay?" he asks.

"For now … you know Paul's gonna start calling you 'Pat the Rat' again, though, right?" he tells him.

"Oh … did he ever really stop?"

"Not really," Matthew admits, kneeling to pick his things off the sidewalk.

"Well, there we go," Patrick laughs, bending down to help.

"You shouldn't have told on him," Matthew says after a moment of silence. "Now he's gonna start beating on you again and making life tough."

Patrick shrugs, but doesn't say anything. He picks up Matthew's inhaler, passing it to him, and tries to unwrinkle some of the crumpled pages by holding them taut and rubbing them over his thigh. Matthew drops the Beclomethasone into the schoolbag, coughing into the crook of his arm, and watches Patrick with a sad frown.

"But thanks, you know, for saving my neck."

"Don't thank me just yet. Don't you have math with him tomorrow afternoon?"

Matthew groans.

"Had to remind me, didn't you?"

With Matthew's belongings collected and packed away, the two boys head down Center Street together in comfortable silence. The early September wind feels good on their skin under the warm rays of the afternoon sun, and Matthew can't help but hope that winter will come late this year. The leaves on the trees are still mostly green, but the tips of yellow and orange foliage peek out from between the branches, and he knows in a few short weeks he'll be back to long sleeves, sweaters, and warm jackets.

"See you tomorrow?"

"You're not going home yet?" Matthew asks, surprised.

"Nah, I'm gonna meet my brothers at the Ash Avenue Boys' Club. Wanna come?"

"Can't. Got that stupid history test tomorrow."

"Oh, okay. Later, Matt."

"Yeah, see ya … And thanks again, eh Patrick?"

Patrick smiles and waves goodbye, heading west on Wellington, and Matthew watches him go for a minute before heading in the opposite direction to his home in Griffintown. He can feel a lump forming in the back of his throat, his eyes suddenly stinging, angry that his best friend—the smallest kid that ever grew up in the Point—was forced to come to his defence today. And as much as he appreciates the help, he knows the beating Paul is gonna give him tomorrow is going to be even worse as a result.

Eyes on the ground, he notices the white rubber toes of his new black running shoes are scuffed, probably from when he hopped the black iron fence. He kicks at a tuft of grass peeking through the cracks of the sidewalk in frustration. As mad as he is at Paul for picking on him, he's angrier at himself for not being faster, for not pushing harder, for letting the two boys catch him day after day after day. He wants to scream in frustration and pull his hair as he thinks of all the other Wednesdays that David and Paul have ruined for him. This year he's finally in grade six, this year he's finally graduating, this year was *supposed* to be different.

But it isn't.

It's just like all the other years before it.

His face feels hot, anger welling up inside him, and he can feel tears threatening to spill over. He grabs the straps of his leather school bag, pulling the bag hard against his back, and he runs.

His feet beat the pavement at full speed, rubber soles slapping against the pavement as he runs down Wellington, the Lachine Canal coming into view. His heart hammers against his ribs, his lungs feel like they're breathing in fire, and the muscles in his legs are sore and quivering as he propels himself down the street. It doesn't take long before his chest begins to tighten, his throat closing up and air getting harder and harder to take in. His sprint slows to a jog, his jog to a walk, and eventually he comes to a complete stop. He stands still, bending at the waist to hang his head between his knees, gulping air as sweat beads off his brow and rolls down his face. He closes his eyes, trying to calm himself without reaching for his inhaler. Eventually his heartbeat slows and his lungs relax.

He continues down the street. Waves beat against the cement walls of the canal, and the sound of the birds overhead mixes with the noise of faraway cars on the highway. He scoops up some pebbles from the side of the road and throws them one at a time over the metal railing, watching them disappear into the blackness of the dirty water. He eyes a pack of ducks drifting along with the stream and stops, takes aim, and throws one of the pebbles with all his strength, imagining Paul's beefy face as he lets the rock fly. It makes its mark, clipping one of the ducks on its rear end and sending it squawking up the canal along with the rest of its paddling.

"Look at 'em go! Great shot!" someone calls out.

Matthew jumps and spins on his heel, trying to spot who's followed him down the empty street.

"I'm over here," the voice calls out again.

Matthew looks out over the canal and, much to his surprise, spots an older boy standing on the edge of the old Wellington swing bridge. The bridge stands abandoned in the middle of the canal, having been shut down in favour of the Wellington Tunnel years ago when the waterway stopped being used for commercial trade. Matthew's father sometimes talks about working on the canal with his own father when he was younger and watching as the operators powered up the pivoting bridge that connects Pointe-Saint-Charles to Griffintown. The entire structure would turn to allow boats up and down the canal, before swinging closed and bisecting the waterway once more.

The boy is leaning against one of the rusted steel beams and smiling across the water at Matthew. A white collared shirt peeks out from underneath his black suit and his pants are cut off at the knee. His black leather shoes reflect the bright afternoon sun.

"Fine aim you got there," the boy calls out, voice echoing against the wall of the basin.

"Thanks," Matthew calls back.

He drops the remaining pebbles onto the ground and resumes walking, eyes fixed on the ground as he begins to make his way past the bridge and the strangely dressed boy.

"What's your name?"

"Matthew."

"Matthew ... ?"

"Massi," he answers, attempting to avert his eyes from the other boy but unable to keep from flicking curious glances at him occasionally.

"Nice to meet you, Matthew Massi. My name's Art. Well, Arthur Carr, but only my ma calls me Arthur," he says, pulling a face. "So, not to be nosy, but why're you throwing rocks at ducks?"

"I wasn't," Matthew grumbles. "I was throwing rocks at Paul."

"You named the duck Paul? That's a dumb name for a duck. What'd Paul do to get you mad at him? Quack too loud?"

"No!" Matthew shouts, stopping in his tracks to glare up at Art in frustration. "I was throwing rocks at this *stupid* kid named Paul. Or, at least, that's what I was imagining ... " he trails off, biting his lip.

"Kid givin' you a hard time?"

"I don't really feel like talking about it," he says with a shrug.

"Oh, okay."

The two stare at each other for a moment in awkward silence before Matthew furrows his brow and points at Art.

"What's wrong with your suit?" Matthew asks.

"Whaddaya mean by that?"

"Nothing! Just, the pants … you're missing the ends of them."

"Cut 'em off."

"Why?"

"It's hot out. Why do you care?"

"I don't … sorry."

Matthew continues to walk down Wellington Street, as Art matches his pace along the old bridge.

"You're headed to the tunnel, aren't you?" Art asks.

"Yeah, it's the quickest way home."

"You live in the Griff?" Art asks, perking up.

"Yeah, on Mountain. You?"

"Me too!" Art cries.

"Really?"

Matthew raises an eyebrow and eyes the boy suspiciously. Even though it's a long street, he knows practically everyone who lives in the area, and this strange looking boy who is filled with too many questions isn't ringing any bells. He quickens his pace.

"Well, I *used* to," Art says sheepishly, speeding up to keep up with the other boy. He runs one hand down the side of his perfectly parted, slicked brown hair while he stuffs the other one into his pocket. "But I haven't been there in a long time."

"How long's it been?"

"Sixty years."

Matthew's frown eases when Art chuckles at his own joke.

"Where do you live now?"

"Here. There. Wherever I want."

Art doesn't tell him out loud, but Matthew knows what he's really saying. *A street kid.* He feels a twinge of pity for the older boy hanging out on the abandoned metal bridge. It might be warm now, but winter is fast on its way and the city can be unforgiving.

"How'd you get up there, anyways?"

"I jumped."

Matthew gapes at him in disbelief and shakes his head.

"No, there's no way. You jumped across all this?" he asks, motioning to the gap between the steel beams and the road.

"No, dummy, I jumped on the bridge when it swung around," he laughs.

Matthew opens his mouth to call Art a liar—the bridge hasn't worked in years—but the other boy continues talking.

"Matt, I really wouldn't take the tunnel if I were you."

"Oh yeah? Why's that?"

"Buncha kids went in there before you came along. Looked like they wanted a fight. If I was you, I'd take the long way home today."

Matthew stops in his tracks and stares off toward the tunnel. It's a gaping hole in the old grey wall, hard to miss even if you don't know where to look, and even though the sun is shining brightly, the entrance to the tunnel looks black. It's only a fifteen minute walk to his duplex from the tunnel, but the thought of walking under the canal in the dark confining space—alone—makes him anxious.

"How many?" he asks.

"What?"

"How many went in?"

"Three, four, I think. I wasn't countin' em'," he says, rolling his eyes.

Matthew considers the situation. Three kids at this hour means it's probably the Mailloux family, and he has nothing to worry about from them. Matthew's mom and his are close, and if they try to pull any- thing they'll get the beating of a lifetime at home. On the other hand, if it's four kids this early in the day then it might be the Frances broth- ers skipping class again, in which case he's in for trouble. That would turn his already sour day even worse.

He could always wait around for Patrick and his brothers. Although Patrick is small and wiry, his two older brothers are massive by any- one's standards. No one in the Point, Griffintown, or even Goose Vil- lage would ever think of picking on the youngest Laprairie son when his two bodyguards are around. As much as he wants to wait for them to finish at the Boys' Club, though, the idea of needing his friend to come to his rescue twice in the same day makes Matthew red with embarrassment, so he continues to make his way toward the tunnel.

"You're gonna go in anyway?" Art asks, surprised. "Didn't take you for the fightin' type."

"I'm not."

"Ohhh," Art says, drawing the sound out. "A runner then. Like your style."

Matthew swallows hard, a familiar knot forming in the back of his throat, and the back of his neck starts feeling hot as he focuses on the tunnel, walking toward it at a brisk pace. Art's right to think he's a runner, but Matthew isn't about to mention that he's not a terribly fast one.

"Good luck!" Art calls after him from his post on the swing bridge. He walks to the edge of the structure and sits down, feet dangling over the water below, and stares after Matthew with a frown.

Matthew approaches the tunnel and walks ramrod straight, his thin shoes beating against the pavement as the blackness of the tunnel swallows him whole. It's colder in the tunnel, which probably shouldn't surprise him, and he feels a chill pass down his spine as the sound of his footsteps echoes through the empty space. The working lights on the walls are dim and do little to lighten the space, and the broken ones flicker and whine. It's a short walk, but in the dark it feels like it goes on forever. As he approaches the end of the tunnel, he can hear the voices of the boys Art was talking about, and dread pools in his stomach as he shields his eyes against the bright afternoon sunlight to count the shadowy figures up ahead.

One, two ... three.

He lets out a sigh of relief as he approaches the boys. It's only when he's halfway through calling out a greeting that he spots the fourth kid, and he immediately wishes he'd taken Art's advice about finding another way home as the Frances boys come into focus.

"Hey Mattie! Why're you so happy to see us?" drawls the youngest boy, feral smile plastered across his face.

Two of the Frances boys enter the tunnel and push past Matthew, standing behind him and preventing him from going back the way he came. The other two stand side by side at the Griffintown exit just up ahead, cutting off his way home. Matthew's palms start to get sweaty, his heart resumes beating at a fast and familiar tempo, and he tries not to look afraid as the boys close in.

"Damn it, Matthew! Do you know how expensive textbooks are? Do you think your mother and I are made of money? We can't keep buying you new books every time you lose one!" his father yells, from across the dinner table.

"Sorry," he says quietly, staring down at his supper. He pushes the meatloaf from one end of his plate to the other with his fork, leaving a trail of gravy through the mashed potatoes, peas, and turnips.

"You don't play with your food, you eat it," his father scolds.

He can feel his older siblings staring at him, attempting to stifle their snickers. Margaret giggles under her breath, and their mother shoots her a quelling look. Thomas and Rebecca manage to stay silent, but their blue eyes are alight with amusement as their father gets increasingly worked up.

"You know money's tight right now, but you still go and pull this shit?" his dad says, stabbing at his plate.

Matthew bites his tongue hard enough to draw blood as he thinks of the new AMC Rambler parked outside the duplex, polished bright enough for his dad to see his reflection in the paint on a cloudy day. He cuts a large piece off his slice of meatloaf with the side of his fork and shovels it into his mouth, chewing on the tasteless ground beef and swallowing it down with difficulty. He picks up his glass of milk and takes a swig to wash it down.

"Mattie, sweetheart, I know you're not *trying* to misplace your things, but you can't keep being this forgetful," his mother says evenly. "You *need* to be more careful. Your father and I can't afford to keep replacing everything you lose."

"We're not buying you a new one, end of story," his father grumbles through a mouthful of turnips.

"I said I was sorry," Matthew protests.

He wants to tell them it wasn't his fault; he wants to tell them the Frances boys took his history book, but he keeps his eyes fixed on his plate and tries not to argue. According to his dad, everything that happened today *was* his fault anyway.

"A boy your age should know how to throw a punch," his father had told him a few years back. It had been the first time Matthew had come crying to him about the boys at school. *"Even if you don't win, you shouldn't be scared to fight. I won't have a coward for a son, no, not under this roof."*

Matthew hadn't dared to bring the boys at school up in conversation again ever since.

"You're going to save up every allowance, every penny, and every cent of birthday money until you can buy yourself another damn book."

"But that's not fair!" Matthew shouts before he can stop himself. "What am I supposed to use until then?"

"Don't you raise your voice to me!" his dad yells, pounding his fists on the table, bits of turnip spraying out of his mouth and speckling his beard. "That's not my damn problem!"

Matthew's hands shake and his eyes feel hot. His mother's sad stare and his siblings' expressions of glee don't help, and he pushes himself to his feet.

"Where do you think you're going?" his father asks quietly.

"I'm not hungry."

"If you leave this table after all the work your mother put into making you a hot dinner, then I better not see you for the rest of the goddamned night. Do you understand me?"

"Yes."

"Yes, what?"

"Yes, *sir*."

Matthew pushes his chair in and storms out of the dining room to his small bedroom. It's a cramped space, hardly enough room for him, let alone all his things. He sits heavily on his bed, balling his hands into fists and pounding them down on his pillow. He imagines that he's hitting his father's and Paul's faces instead of the lime green bedding. When he tires of this, he stares out the small window that overlooks the laneway behind the rundown duplex. He watches the neighbour's dog bark at people who aren't there, watches the shadows of people moving through their homes behind closed curtains, watches as the sun finally begins to set in the evening sky.

He lies down on his bed and stares up at the ceiling. It takes him a long time, but eventually he falls into a dreamless sleep.

"Matt, that seems like a *really* bad idea," Patrick says as the two boys change out of their gym uniforms into their day clothes. "You're gonna get yourself killed."

"Not if I leave *right* as the bell rings," Matt replies, pulling on his tan slacks. "I don't even have to go back to my locker," he adds proudly, holding up his book bag, which he'd crammed into the small gym locker.

"Okaaaay ... "

"And, think about it, Paul definitely won't follow us if we go this way."

"I wonder why!"

"If you don't want to come—"

"I don't, Matt, I *really* don't."

Patrick is afraid, looking smaller than usual, and Matthew can't blame him; the idea of cutting through the French school is enough to give any Anglo second thoughts.

"That's okay, Patrick, you don't have to," he says, with a small smile. "You gonna be okay to get home though?"

"Yeah. My brothers are meeting me after school, and we're going to Hogan's Bath. You wanna come?"

Matthew shakes his head.

"You sure? Swimming sure beats, well, getting a beating."

"It's gonna be fine," Matthew says, smiling wide as the bell rings loudly. "Later, Patrick!"

Matthew takes off through the dreary white halls of Canon O'Meara, pushing past other students to the front door, and barreling down the steps before anyone else. He runs up Island Street to Saint Patrick, turning the corner fast onto Seigneurs and running full speed into the kid in front of him. The two go sprawling onto the sidewalk.

"*Crisse!*" the other boy shouts, pushing himself up off the ground, as a circle of school kids forms around them. The boy's lip is split, and his arm looks red and sore from where he slid on the ground.

"I'm really sorry," Matthew says, breathing hard. He rolls himself into a sitting position and examines the damage. His slacks and skin are torn on his right knee, blood beginning to stain the fabric. His hands and chin are scraped from where he landed, and his ankle is sore.

"*Maudit tête carré!*" the boy yells, and Matthew realizes—with some horror—that he's run into a pack of students from the French school.

He pushes himself up onto his feet and tries to make a break for it, but one of the boys cuffs him in the ear, putting him off balance, and sends him sprawling back onto the sidewalk. Two other boys pull Matthew to his feet, and the boy he ran into throws a punch that connects hard with his left eye. Matthew yells and kicks blindly at the kid, his foot and sore ankle making contact, and the kid shouts in pain. The two boys holding him up let him go, then one of them shoves Matthew hard to the ground.

Matthew lands, cursing under his breath, but manages to push himself to his feet before anyone can land a kick. He runs, ankle threatening to buckle underneath him, heading back down Saint Patrick Street and the relative safety of the English school district.

"Pepsi May West!" he screams over his shoulder, spitting at the boys who aren't far behind him.

Spotting Canon O'Meara in the distance, the French schoolboys begin to fall back.

"*Ciboire!*" one of them shouts.

Matthew limps along Saint Patrick as he makes his way toward the tunnel for the second time that week. Once on Wellington, he begins to lean against the metal railing by the canal for support, trying to avoid putting weight on his ankle.

"You look like you went a round with Joe Gans," Art calls out from the swing bridge as Matthew approaches.

"Who?"

"A boxer, one of the best in the world," he says excitedly, jumping in place and jabbing at the air.

"Never heard of him."

Art lowers his fists and frowns. "Well, anyway, what happened? That louse Paul givin' you a hard time again?"

"Yeah, well, no."

"Which is it?"

Matthew stops and leans against the banister, tired of walking on his sore leg.

"Both, I guess. I didn't want Paul razzing on me again, so I cut through where the French kids go to school. And, well, they didn't like that too much … especially when I knocked one of them over."

Art bursts into laughter, doubled over and clutching his stomach. Eventually the laughter dies down and he stares out at Matthew, wiping a tear out of his eye.

"Matt, you goop! You gotta be batty to cut through the Frenchies' school."

"My friend Patrick said the same thing."

"Your friend Pat's gotta head on his shoulders. Why'd you do something so boneheaded anyway?"

"I was trying to get home quicker. Didn't want to take the tunnel again, and crossing through Seigneurs to Basin is the fastest way to Mountain. Plus, you know, Paul wasn't about to follow me that way."

Art nods and unbuttons his suit jacket. He leans against one of the metal beams, letting the rays of the sun light up his face. Matthew takes a seat on the pavement, legs straddling one of the metal bars, and the two boys look across the water at each other.

"Didn't really work out the way I thought it would, to be honest."

"You don't say," Art drawls. "Why don't you take the bridge?"

"What bridge?"

"This bridge, dummy," Art laughs.

Matthew furrows his brow and stares at the massive structure in the water.

"It's the easiest way to get from the Point to the Griff, so why're you takin' the long way 'round?"

"Because the bridge hasn't worked in years. Which reminds me, you never did tell me how you get up on there."

"Yes I did! I told you, I jumped when the bridge was swinging."

"But that's impossible. The bridge hasn't—"

"Been *used* for years. Doesn't mean that it doesn't still work. The controls are here," Art points vaguely to what looks like a rusted metal box on the manmade platform. "I can swing it around for you, if you want. That way you won't have to take the tunnel again today, and we can hang out here for a bit!"

"I don't know … It doesn't really look all that safe."

"Aww, come on! I'm up here, aren't I? You'll be fine."

"Nah. Plus, I should really be getting home."

"Oh, you don't have to leave yet. You only just got here."

The look he gives Matthew is almost pleading, and Matthew realizes with a twinge of sadness that Art probably doesn't have many friends.

"Yeah, I guess I can stick around … "

"D'you have a hard time in the tunnel yesterday?"

Matthew sighs, wishing they could talk about anything else, but he finally gives in and tells Art about what happened the day before, about how useless he felt, and about what his father had said to him at dinner.

"What a rat," Art says angrily. "It's not your fault there were four of them."

"Don't tell him that."

"You don't get along with him? Your dad."

Matthew shrugs.

"It's okay. I hate my old man, too. Or, I did. He died a while back."

Art pauses, expecting Matthew to interject, and continues when the other boy remains silent.

"I always liked swimmin'. Wanned to be a bigshot speed swimmer. I was faster than everyone I knew, and this club was looking to take on new racers, so I wanned to be one of 'em. Got a membership to the Montreal Swimming Club and everythin'. So, the day of tryouts, what does my pa do? He starts wailin' on me, yellin' I don't pull my weight, sayin' I'm a burden on the rest of 'em. The bastard clouts me hard on the ear," Art tells him sadly, "and I think he maybe popped it or somethin', 'cause my balance was shot afterward, but I didn't care. I needed to make the swim meet. So I'm runnin', stumblin' over myself, and I get to this bridge, and I jump … "

"And?" Matthew asks, holding his breath.

"Nothin'. I just … I didn't make it in time. Never got on the swim team."

Neither of them speaks for a while, the sound of the water lapping against the side of the Lachine Canal filling the silence between them.

"I'm sorry," Matthew finally offers.

"Don't be," Art says, looking out on the horizon. "I'm glad he's gone."

"You don't miss him?"

"No," Art laughs, "but I miss … I don't know. I miss havin' someone to play with, I guess."

The two sit in comfortable silence for a long time. So long, in fact, that it's only the sound of rush hour traffic that reminds Matthew that he needs to get home.

"I'll see you tomorrow?" he asks, as he gets up.

"You know where to find me."

Matthew tugs on the laces of his scuffed shoes, trying not to cringe as the fabric pulls against his scraped hands, and ties his runners tight. His black eye is swollen nearly shut, and his ankle hurts to even look at, but he's not going to let anyone have the satisfaction of seeing him in pain. Least of all Paul.

He'd failed the history test the day before—just like he knew he would without the textbook—and his teacher made him stay late this afternoon to write lines as punishment, hoping to drill the right answers into his head for the next test. Unfortunately, it didn't take long for Paul and his lackey to find out that Matthew was going to be walking home alone on Friday night, and Matthew can see the boy's hulking form waiting for him outside the front gate of the school.

He rummages through his bag for his Beclomethasone. He finds the brown inhaler and shakes it well before taking a hit. He puts the medication back in his bag, which he slings across his back, and prepares himself for the long run home.

He knows he's not going to make it, but that's not going to stop him from trying.

He opens the heavy front door, letting it slam closed behind him, and starts walking down the front path of Canon O'Meara. Paul grins, something predatory in the way his thin lips curl as he walks toward the iron fence.

"Came out to play after all, eh Mattie?"

He waits for an answer, but Matthew doesn't say anything as he calmly approaches the gate.

"You're gonna be eating through a tube after this knuckle sandwich."

Paul pulls his fist back, and that's when Matthew runs. He pushes David with all his strength and bolts past the two boys with all the speed he can muster. His feet pound the pavement, waves of pain shooting through his ankle and up his leg as he charges down Center Street. He can hear David hot on his heels, along with Paul's laboured breathing as he hunts Matthew down. Matthew's chest is tight, lungs taking in less and less air, but he refuses to stop as he turns onto Wellington. In the distance he can see the swing bridge, and Art's silhouette against the darkening sky.

"You're ... dead ... Mattie!" Paul shouts between pants, his face red with exertion.

Matthew glances over his shoulder, sees that David is gaining on him, and begins to panic. He knows that in a few short moments the larger boy will be on top of him, giving him the beating of a lifetime. He knows that if he's caught, this year will be a repeat of the year before, and the year before that. He'll be a punching bag every day for the rest of the year, afraid to go anywhere alone, forced to wait for Patrick and his brothers every day and hoping that Paul will finally get tired of terrorizing him and move on to another victim.

The Wellington Bridge is closer now, Art pacing along the edge of it as he watches Matthew run.

"Swing … it!" he screams to Art. He runs with all his might, his muscles screaming, trying to ignore the sound of David closing in on him.

There's a loud groan, heavy steel scraping against heavy steel, and Matthew watches in astonishment as the bridge begins to pivot in the Lachine Canal, seemingly of its own volition. The rusted structure slowly spins towards the road and Art stands atop it, motioning for Matthew to run faster.

How is he controlling it? Isn't the control box … ?

"Get ready to jump! Matt, you have to go now!" Art screams from the end of the bridge.

Matthew beelines for the metal railing of the canal. He runs, pushing himself to his limits as he approaches the banister. He launches himself over the railing of the canal, just like he's done so many times with the gate of Canon O'Meara, and throws himself at the bridge with the last of his strength. As he pushes off the wall, his ankle buckles underneath him, and he knows right away he won't make the jump like he should.

He falls, grabbing desperately for the bridge, and manages to cling to a metal beam just below the ledge. His torn hands ache, and panic floods his senses as the bridge moves him slowly closer to the concrete wall. Above him on the street, he can hear David and Paul screaming for help.

He looks up and sees Art leaning comfortably against the rusting steel.

"Pull me up!" he yells, voice cracking. "Art, help me up!"

Art smiles and crosses his arms over his chest as he watches Matthew dangle helplessly over the water.

"Help me up!"

Matthew looks over his shoulder. The solid cement wall is only a few feet away.

"Arthur, help me up!"

"It's *Art*. And if I do, you'll go back to your crummy life with your crummy dad and the crummy kids from school. But if I don't, I won't be alone, and you won't have to keep runnin'. Don't worry, Matt, it only hurts for a second. Promise."

"What?" Matthew cries, the wall inches from his skin. "What are you saying? Help me, Art!"

"I am."

Matthew stares up at him, bile building in the back of his throat.

"So I'm runnin', stumblin' over myself, and I get to this bridge, and I jump ... I didn't make it in time. Never got on the swim team."

Art smiles down at him, and Matthew closes his eyes. Cold cement presses against his skin from one side as the hard steel crushes him from the other. His chest is tight—different than all the other times—and he opens his mouth to scream.

With a deafening thud the Wellington Bridge clicks into place against the wall, and everything is silent.

2015

Sarah wipes a tear away with the back of her hand, hoping her eyes don't look as puffy as they feel. Her phone vibrates in her pocket, and, with some reluctance, she takes it out and answers it.

"Where are you? You were supposed to be home an hour ago!" the voice screams on the other end of the line.

"I know, Mom. Sorry."

"What happened?"

"Jody hid all my clothes again after gym. I couldn't find them, and by the time I did, the school bus had already gone," she says, throat tight. "I'll be home in the next hour or so—I'm headed to the overpass now."

"You couldn't take the city bus?"

"No … you didn't fill my *OPUS* card this month … "

"So it's my fault you're not on time, then? Is that what you're telling me?"

"No, of course not, Mom. I'm sorry," Sarah says, quietly.

"I need you home. *Now.* Your brothers need help with their home-work, I don't know where the fuck your dad is, and I need to get to work. So get home. Got it?"

"Yeah, got it. Bye, Mom."

She hangs up her phone and puts it back in her pocket, staring at the ground as she makes the long trip to the overpass connecting Pointe-Saint-Charles to Griffintown. It's a quiet afternoon, the only noise the sound of traffic in the distance and the waves of the canal splashing against the basin walls.

"You're headed to the overpass, aren't you?" a boy calls out.

Sarah looks behind her, startled, but doesn't see anyone.

"I'm over here," the boy calls out again.

She turns, spotting two boys watching her as they lean against the rusted steel beams of the old swing bridge. One is dressed in a peculiar black suit cut at the knees, and the other is wearing vintage-looking clothes with scuffed black sneakers. The boy in the sneakers waves as she stares back at him.

"Yeah, it's the quickest way home," she says.

"You live in the Griff?" the boy asks excitedly.

"Yeah, on William Street."

"Me too!" he cries.

"Really?"

"Yeah, but I wouldn't take the overpass if I were you."

"And why's that?" she asks.

"Bunch of guys headed that way before you came along. Looked like they weren't too keen on making friends. If I was you, I'd find another way home today. But don't worry, I know a shortcut into the Griff, if you want."

She nods, nervous, and he smiles at her.

"What's your name?"

"Sarah."

"Sarah … ?"

"Rosenthal," she answers.

"Nice to meet you, Sarah Rosenthal. My name's Matthew, but you can call me Matt."

Stuck

Originally published in Sanitarium Magazine no. 19, *March 2014.*

Beep! Beep! Beep! Beep!

The alarm sounds off loudly in my room, the noise echoing down the hall towards me. My brain feels fuzzy. I must've nodded off on the couch sometime last night. The stupid thing's more comfortable than my bed. Best damn purchase I've made since buying an apartment across town from my ex. He never would've let me buy a leather sofa. He used to say the material would stick to his legs if he wore boxers, and that it would heat up like an oven if the sun got it. He used to say a lot of things I didn't agree with. So I don't care about him or his sticky legs anymore.

I don't feel like getting up, I don't want to move, but the noise is making me crazy. I open my eyes... are they already open? The room looks blurry and out of focus. My eyes feel dry, sore, and I'm so tired. I didn't know people could sleep with their eyes open. I've never done that before, or I don't think I've done that before. It doesn't seem like something I've done.

I go to blink, but I don't. Why don't I blink? I try to do it again, but nothing happens. It feels like there's dust in my eyes, and I want them to water. Nothing happens. Something should be happening. Why isn't something happening? I'm still trying to blink without success. The alarm is still ringing, and now I want to turn it off. I will myself to blink, but it's impossible. I try to roll my eyes, but they're still. Something's wrong. Really wrong. I'm pulling down on my eyelids with as much mental force as I can, but it's not working. Why isn't it working?

Are my eyes broken? That doesn't make sense; eyes don't break, or they don't break like this. I don't understand, why aren't they moving? Why isn't anything else moving? My heart should be racing, but it isn't. I can't hear it doing anything. Is my heart beating? It has to be, because I'm here panicking, but I can't hear it. Did I go deaf? No, I'm not deaf. I can still hear that fucking alarm. I really need to turn it off.

I go to get up, but I can't get up. I can't move. I should be moving. Why am I not moving? Am I paralyzed? Maybe I fell asleep wrong. Maybe I fell asleep with my head resting awkwardly, and then when I turned in the night, I pulled a nerve or snapped my own neck. Did I snap my own neck? Is that even possible? That can't be possible! I don't remember snapping my own neck, but I don't remember falling asleep either.

Beep! Beep! Beep! Beep!

Oh my god. Oh my god. Move. Move! Just move! Pull an Uma Thurman and wiggle your big toe. Easy peasy. I'm giving it my all, but it's not moving. No matter how hard I try to move my toe, blink an eye, my body doesn't want to listen to my brain. They've been disconnected, separated, and I can't do anything about it. I need help.

I try to call out, but I can't move my lips. My tongue feels heavy and big. It's like a limp piece of meat stuck in my dry mouth. I can't say a word. Just like I can't stop looking up at my damn ceiling or listening to my stupid alarm clock. I try to make a sound, try to push air from my lungs up into my throat. I'll settle for a gurgle, even a ghost of a noise, but the room stays quiet. I stay quiet.

This is a dream. This has to be a dream. This isn't real because it can't be real. People don't just wake up one morning to find themselves stuck. It's definitely a dream. A very scary, a very real, a very horrible dream. I want to wake up. How do I wake up?

Bang! Bang! Bang!

Bang? My alarm clock never bangs. What's banging and why isn't the noise waking me up? Maybe this isn't a dream, maybe this is real. This can't be real, but I think it is. There it goes again, more banging. There's muffled shouting, but I don't know who's shouting. I recognize the voice, but I can't remember. My head is still fuzzy, and it feels like sleep is trying to pull me away. Except I don't want to go away, I want to stay here. I need to stay here. I need to fix this.

Bang! Bang! Bang!

I know this banging! It's a hard fist hitting the harder drywall. The walls of the complex are thinner than rice paper, and every night I can hear my roid-rage neighbour sleeping with the girlfriend of his roommate that works night shifts. If I can hear them, they can hear me. They can hear the alarm clock, and they can come help me.

"Dude! Can you shut that fucking thing off? Some of us work evenings, jackass!"

Nightshift neighbour! No, I can't turn it off. I can't do anything. I need you to come help me. Please, come and help me! Get the landlord, or get the fire axe and chop down my door. I don't care what you do, just do something. There's more banging, but then it stops. It's been stopped for a long time. Did he get the landlord, or the maintenance guy who stares at people?

BANG! BANG! BANG!

It's at my front door. The door ten feet behind this couch. There's someone ten feet from me, and they can help me. Stop hitting my door and get someone. The alarm stops. It shouldn't stop. I know it turns off on its own after a while to preserve power, or in case someone forgets to unplug it when they go on vacation, but it can't have been long enough for it to give up. Don't give up! Keep yelling at me! Keep yelling at the neighbour! Don't give up on me yet, I still need your help. Isn't the point of an alarm to get you up? So get me up!

The neighbour's footsteps seem farther away. Don't go away! Please don't go away! No, come back. You can't leave, I need you here. I need your help. His door closes. Why are you closing your door? You should be here, yelling at me for waking you up, not going back to bed. Please don't go back to bed.

Everything's so quiet. I'm so quiet. I can't feel my pulse, and my heart should be thumping against my ribcage in fear. My palms should be sweaty, and my chest should be heaving, but they're not. I can't feel my chest rising, or falling. Am I paralyzed? If I was, I wouldn't be able to feel, right? And I can't feel, or I don't think I can feel. I must have snapped my neck. I can't believe I snapped my neck. But I did, or I think I did. No, I did. I definitely did.

How are they going to fix this? Can they fix this? I don't want to be stuck in a motorized wheelchair for the rest of my life, with my brain plugged into a machine that tells my body when to blink and swallow. I don't want to spend the rest of my life eating from a tube. How am I going to work? Public relations means having to talk, and if I can't talk, I can't work. I need to work, it's my life. They'll just have to fix me.

There's a tiny bell. A soft clinking of metal on metal, making its way towards me. Deliberately. I can see a tuft of white fur out the corner of my eye. It moves out of my line of vision, but then all at once appears in front of me. There's a light pressure on my chest from where it's standing and the little bastard doesn't even bother to sheath its claws. It's looking down at me. My cat. Actually, Charles' old cat that I ended up with is looking down at me. He got all the appliances, and I got his stupid fucking cat. Why is it purring? It always hated me too much to show affection. It rubs its face against my chest, and I know it's getting its ugly white fur on me. It's still purring. Stop purring.

It looks me in the eye, and even though cats can't smile, I'm sure it's smiling. It looks too happy to be doing anything else. It knows I'm here, helpless, and it's enjoying it. The furry little fucker is actually enjoying this. I hate cats. They eat their owners if the owner's dead and the cat's out of food. But he has plenty of food, and I'm not dead.

So why does the cat look like it's licking its lips? If it eats me, I'll kill it. Get off of me. Get the hell off me, bitch!

It leans in and licks my cheek. It's not cute, it's not sweet, it's a taste test. The cat's sampling me for later, wetting its chops in anticipation. It wants me to die here so that it can eat me, not out of necessity, but out of fun. It's looking at me like a lion looks at a gazelle that's been taken down by the pride. It licks me again, its whiskers brushing against the side of my nose. Get off of me, you ungrateful, hairball hacking, catnip loving, sneaky little …

That's a key. That's a key being put into a lock. My lock. My lock, on my door. Someone's about to come in and save me. The hinges moan in protest as the door slowly swings open. Who is it? I can't see who it is.

"Shina, you home?"

Yes! I'm home! David, I'm here. Walk forward and look down. That's where I am. Find me. Come over here and find me!

"I saw your car in the parking lot, so I figured you'd still be here. And, because I have a late start this morning, I thought you might be in the mood for breakfast out, or something, if you had the time."

He makes his way forward, slowly. I can hear the soft ticking of his watch. I'd recognize that ticking anywhere. It's from the old watch he wears everywhere, no matter how outdated it is. It's the same one I saw him wearing at the company Christmas party my husband had dragged me to. David worked as a sales rep back then. He still does.

"Shina?"

Even when he isn't looking for me to answer him, he always says my name like it's a question. I can't help but wonder if he has a hard time remembering it. Maybe his wife's name is on the tip of his tongue, ready to jump out of his mouth when he least expects it. I hope mine does when he's with her. At least it'll finally give him a reason to leave her. The same reason his name gave me to divorce Charles. My husband. No, my ex.

He shakes me, and my head rolls uselessly from side to side. He shakes me harder. I can't answer him, I try to, but I can't. I want to scream, cry, fucking blink, but I can't do anything. He takes my face between his hands, and stares into my eyes. He looks desperate, wild. Why hasn't he called for an ambulance? Why is he just looking at me? You can't do anything, so get someone who can. Help me!

He drops my face and backs away quickly. Now pick up the phone, and call 911. He looks at me, horrified, breathing fast. Pick up the phone, David! He wipes his hands on his suit jacket madly, like he's trying to erase me from his skin. What are you doing? Why aren't you calling? He sits down on the window ledge, and puts his head between his knees, breathing deep. He takes out his phone. Good, call. He dials a number. The number's more than three numbers. Who are you calling? Call fucking 911! He waits for them to answer. I wait for him to help me.

"Rick? Rick! Fuck, man, I need your help. I don't know what to do. I'm so fucking screwed. You know that chick I've been banging?"

Chick you've been banging? Chick? Me, it's me, Shina! I'm not some chick, I'm the woman you said you were supposed to end up with. I'm the woman you said you'd leave everything for, not some slut you've been sleeping with.

"She's dead. She's fucking dead."

I'm what? I'm not dead. I'm not dead. I can't be dead, I'm here. I'm here you idiot! I'm right here, I'm talking to you! I just can't move, that's all. I've broken my neck and I can't do anything. I can't speak, but I'm not dead. I'm not. No. I'm here, I'm alive. I need help. I can't be dead! People don't just die like this! I didn't die like this!

"I'm at her place right now, and I don't know what to do. If I call an ambulance, they're going to ask what I'm doing here. They're going to ask how I got in, why I have a key … Fuck. And if Elizabeth finds out, then we're over."

I'm not dead! I can't be dead, because it doesn't make sense. I'm fine. I'm not fine, but I'm not dead. Maybe I'm dead. No, I'm not. I'm just stuck, just trapped. I just can't move. I'm not dead. I'm dead. No I'm not!

"I don't want to lose her, Rick. I just, I just don't know what to do."

You don't want to lose her? You told me you were leaving her! You're not leaving her? I'm not dead. We're over. Once I'm fixed, we're over. And I'll be fine, because I'm right here, I'm alive, and we're over.

He hangs up the phone, and takes a long pause before calling 911. He lies to them. He tells them I'm dead on my couch, but that's not true. I know it's not true. When he hangs up, he puts the phone down on the coffee table and just watches me. Why are you watching me?

Stop watching me. I don't want you looking at me, and I can't look away from you.

This is the man I used as my excuse? You were the reason I got a divorce? I knew my marriage was heading nowhere fast, but to give it all up for you? Charles may not have loved me, but he wouldn't be useless like you. He wouldn't give up trying. I don't think he ever did give up trying. What's he going to say when he finds out I'm dead. Not dead, paralyzed?

How are you going to tell him, David? Are you going to say we were just friends, and that you were meeting me for breakfast? What kind of lie are you going to come up with, to explain your key? Or are you too worried about losing your job? You're pathetic. I can't wait until they fix me. I can't wait to take apart the lies you're going to invent, or to tell Charles that it was you I slept with. And I will tell them, because I'm fine.

I will be fine.

Except, I'm starting to think I'm really dead. I can't hear my own breath, or feel my heartbeat. I can't move and I feel cold. I can't be dead, but I feel dead. I'm not dead ... probably. Why is it taking so long for them to come and help me? The ambulance should be here by now. Why isn't it here yet?

I can hear footsteps from the hall. Who is it? Is it the paramedics? I can hear them talking to each other. They're getting closer. I'm in here! David hears them and gets up to go meet them at the door. They're all coming closer now, but none of them seem to hurry. They need to hurry because I need them to help me. They need to fix this.

The one with the skinnier face comes close to me and shines a light in my eye. I stare straight into it. He puts a finger on my wrist, waiting to feel my pulse. He frowns. Don't frown. He looks back at the other one, and they roll the stretcher closer to the couch. Good! They know I'm broken, and that they need to hurry to reverse this. One of them leaves to get something from the truck. Shouldn't they have everything they need with them? The rat faced one calls it in to the dispatcher.

They're bringing in a body.

That's not right. It's not. I'm not a body. I'm alive. Why can't they get it right? Why can't I hear my heart? The other one comes back from the ambulance with something black. He lays it on the stretcher while the other one consoles David. Then he unzips it and I realize it's a bag. It's a body bag. It's my body bag. I'm not dead!

They slide the stretcher next to the sofa and place me on top of it. Don't put me in the bag. Please don't put me in the bag. Please. Please! Oh god, I'll do anything not to go in that bag. There's a mistake, a big mistake. They wrap the edges of the bag around me, the cold plastic rubbing against my skin. Don't do it. But they're doing it.

They zip the bag almost closed, leaving only my face out of the plastic. The rat-faced paramedic comes closer and reaches his gloved hand out towards me. What are you doing? He puts it on my eyelids and begins to close my eyes. Stop! I want him to stop but he's not stopping. My eyes are closed, and everything's too dark. I want to scream. I can't scream, but I'm still trying.

They're rolling me down the hall. I can't hear David anymore. Is he still in the apartment? I can't hear much over the sound of their heavy boots on the floor. I catch snippets of them talking. They're discussing hockey scores and Chinese food. The wheels on the stretcher squeak, and my body slides forwards a bit when they accidentally roll me into the elevator wall. How can these gorillas in work boots be so careless? They pull me along until the floor becomes too bumpy to be a floor. It's pavement. I'm outside. Cars are rushing by and people are talking in low voices, or I think I can hear people talking. They shove me into the back of the ambulance and slam the doors shut.

I can't hear anything anymore. Everything's quiet. No, the engine revs. They're driving. We're going to the hospital. The back cabin is filled with the clinks of machinery and emergency response equipment bumping around. Are we stopping for coffee? I can't tell for sure, but I think they just stopped for coffee. They still haven't put the sirens on. They still think I'm dead, and I'm starting to think they're right, but they can't be right, because I don't want them to be.

The ride to the hospital takes forever. They wheel me down the halls, and into another elevator. The plastic still feels cold, and this gurney keeps whining and creaking. They push me through the doors of another room. There's no sound except a faint humming. Why do I know that sound? They come to a halt and I hear a door being pulled open. It's a sucking kind of sound at first, and then I recognize the noise. My fridge. They're dumping me in a morgue. They're putting me in the people friendly version of a big Maytag.

My back is put onto a freezing slab of steel. They're making a mistake, but I can't tell them. I can't do anything. They slide me into the cubby. I want to cry for them to stop. I want to cry. I don't belong here! The walls radiate cold and I'm shivering. Except I'm not shivering, I just feel like I should be. The door closes behind me, and I'm left alone with nothing but the humming. The humming and the cold.

I'm healthy. I work out, I eat right. I've never had a history of heart disease, or anything for that matter. Unless you count chronic failed relationships as a medical condition, which I don't. How could I have died? I was fine when I went to bed. I wasn't feeling faint, or sick, or different. I was just plain old me, falling asleep. Now I'm here, in a fridge. Alone. Oh god. What if everyone in this fridge is like me too? What if they're all stuck and screaming, but no one can hear them, either?

I'm in the cold for a long time and then someone comes for me. I hear the sucking sound of my compartment door, and the high-pitched scraping of metal being pulled out. My bag is opened, and the warmer air feels nice on my skin. I'm transferred to another gurney and then another metal slab. Where are they moving me?

Someone is taking my clothing off. Why are they stripping me? Stop it! Get off of me! I can feel the cold scissors gliding against my skin as they hack away at my dress. The man sings along with rock songs from the '80s. There's something wrong.

Something's wrong! It hurts! He's cutting into me. Oh god, stop it! Stop! It hurts! He's slicing my chest open. He drags the knife deep through my skin, ripping it open from my chest to my navel. Please make it stop. Just stop it! You'll kill me!

He puts something cold and metal in my chest, and hums to Bon Jovi as he uses it to pull my ribs apart. He's killing me. He's tearing me apart and I can't even scream. Stop! Stop! Stop! STOP! His hands are in me and he's playing with my organs. He's pulling them out! Stop pulling them out! I listen to the wet splatter of something from inside me slapping against the metal table. I'm in hell. I'm dead, and this is my hell. I'm in agony and he doesn't care. He's mutilating me and no one cares. Why isn't anyone stopping him?

A power saw. I can hear it before I can feel it. He's cutting deep into my temple. I want to die. I want it to stop. I want him to stop sawing into my skull, to stop cutting me to ribbons. But it doesn't stop, and I know I'm really dead. I should be unconscious, but I'm not. I can feel everything, and I'm still here. So I'm dead. Dead and trapped.

It finally stops. He sews me up, and washes me down before putting me back in the fridge, naked and sore. The next person who takes me out is the mortician who's going to make me look pretty before they put me in the ground. She brushes out my hair while talking on the phone. She tells whoever's on the other end that she wishes she had my eyebrows. I want to tell her that I wish I had more time. She tells them that it was a cerebral aneurysm that killed me. A blood vessel in my brain must have broken when I fell asleep, and I bled to death internally. She does my nails and applies enough makeup to keep L'Oreal employed for the next ten years. She layers it on so thick that it feels more like paste than foundation. She wrestles a dress onto me.

It feels like the canary yellow one Charles bought me on our honeymoon to Paris. It's completely inappropriate and beyond uncomfortable. I'm going to be buried in a dress I hate, with caked-on foundation. If I was alive, I'd probably die of embarrassment.

They set me up in a casket holding flowers that don't smell real. People shuffle into the room, awkwardly. All of them talk of how much a shock my death is. They don't understand how someone as young as I am can drop dead like that. I don't understand how I dropped dead like that. I want more time. I should have more time! Old people are supposed to be here, not me. Everyone says they're upset, but I don't hear anyone wailing over my body, begging me to come back to them.

"He must be so upset. He really loved her," someone close to me, Jess, says.

"Yeah. The dress Charles picked out for her is beautiful. Someone told me it's the one she wore on their first date," another girl says. I can't tell who it is. Whoever told them about the dress is wrong; I wore jeans on that date.

"He must be so devastated. You know, he never saw the divorce coming," says Jess again. Is it Jess? It might be Dana. They sound exactly alike.

Didn't see it coming? He knew we were getting a divorce before I did. He told me he could feel the distance growing between us for a long time. Who told her he didn't see it coming? Who told them about the dress? They're getting their facts wrong.

"I still can't believe she was sleeping with David," says the mystery woman, "and for him not to even turn up for her funeral..."

David isn't here? After everything, he's not here? He told me he loved me and he can't even come out to this?

"I know! When Charles found out... You should've seen his face. I think he always wanted her to come back to him. I think he knew he made a mistake ending it with her, and he was waiting for her to realize that too."

They move away, talking to themselves. My friends, still gossiping about me, even after I'm gone. No, after I'm dead. I'm not gone. I'm still right here. Right here, and wishing I could go back. I wish I could undo it all with David. I'm not saying Charles and I would've been happy, or even married much longer than we were, but at least David wouldn't have been my reason for ending things. He wouldn't have been the one I was so quick to toss it all away for.

"It's such a shame, that's such a beautiful dress. Do you think they could cremate her in something else," someone jokes as they walk by my body.

Cremate? I'd always wanted to be buried in the same cemetery as my parents. What do they mean, cremate? I don't want to be set on fire. It's a mistake. Just another wrong fact, like the one about my dress. That's all.

Except it isn't a mistake.

I can hear the crackling of fire as they open the door to push me in. My feet are warm, unpleasantly so. There's one hard push, and then the loud clang of the door closing behind me. The fire crackles beneath me. I must be on a grate, or a shelf. Something to let the fire up and let me slip through to the bottom. It's hot. Too hot.

The fire is closer now, and I can smell the coffin burning. I can smell my skin burning. I can feel my skin burning! I want to tell Charles I'm sorry. I want to do a lot of things that I'll never get to. It gets hotter, and I feel my skin crackle and burn, flaking off into ash. The flames devour my body, breaking it into a million flakes of dust. I try to scream.

But everything stays quiet.

The Water

Originally published in Not Just a Pretty Face: Women of Horror

Vol. 1, *May 2020.*

Thump. Thump. Thump. Thump.

Amélie runs fast, her feet pounding against the asphalt in time with her heart, blood pumping hot through her veins. Her legs are heavy and sore from the effort. Her lungs burn as they suck in the cold morning air and spit out heat through her pursed lips. Her muscles work hard to push and pull her body—heavy with exhaustion—forward, determined to reach its destination in record time. She stares at the brown bench near the edge of the canal as she charges forward, gaze fixed unwaveringly on its hard plastic body that's been painted brown to look like wood,.

Only when she's a few short feet from the seat does she extend her hands and brace for impact. Her palms slap hard against it and she holds onto the bench for all she's worth—*stay away from the water*—as the soles of her running shoes slide on the rough ground while she comes to a full stop a few feet from the railing bordering the water. She stops the timer on her watch, checking the results, and lets out a lacklustre "Whoo!" between gasps for air at beating her old time. Despite her seemingly underwhelming enthusiasm, and the muscle pain now radiating throughout her body, Amélie's proud of her success.

When she first told Théo that she was going to get a morning run in before her shift at the hospital, he laughed until he was blue in the face. A night owl, her job was early enough that she already had trouble rolling out of bed in the morning, so the thought of her getting up even before that was comical. But, even more determined to work out, and desperate to prove him wrong, she'd managed to drag herself out the door at quarter after five each morning for the last two months.

While she quickly got accustomed to being up before the sun, it took her a while to settle on a jogging route. Although she loved being in the heart of downtown, and being close to all the amenities big city life brought, it quickly became apparent that one of the things it *didn't* include was space to stretch her legs alone. Her first day out of the apartment resulted in way more human contact than she was prepared for at that hour of the day, and her second day wasn't much better. By the end of week one she'd accidentally joined a mommy-to-be running club and discovered that most of the solo running paths through the city forced her to trek at least halfway up Mount Royal to get her kilometres in.

Then Théo suggested the canal.

At first, she'd been horrified at the suggestion, refusing to speak to him at all for the rest of the day, and refusing to talk about his suggestion for a lot longer than that.

Stay away from the water, Amélie.

Her *grand maman* had told her stories of the Lachine Canal when she was a child. A man-made waterway from the 1800s, it facilitated trade into Montréal and had become a major tourist attraction in the years following its completion. At night, in the Old Port, it was especially popular, with its rows of vendors in their red huts made from repurposed storage containers, twinkling lights wrapped around the railings mounted on the high walls lining the edge of the water, and pubs advertising cheap food and cheaper beer. During the summer, the walkways were packed with artists and musicians finding inspiration, and in the winter it was the go-to place for everyone celebrating *Nuit Blanche*.

Except for Amélie.

Because while everyone else was talking about how beautiful the stars were, high above the water, she was too busy thinking of the men who lined the trench beneath them.

The men who died digging. The men crushed beneath heavy stones, concrete, and steel beams as water filled the once empty canal. The men and women who died along the water's edge, quarantined from the city as tuberculosis killed them in isolation, their broken bodies thrown into the canal to keep the ailing of the city safe. The runaways from the Point, the children abandoned from the Griff, the teenage addicts from the West, all finding refuge in the canal when all they wanted was to go home.

They can never go home, no matter how much they try. Stay away from the water, Amélie.

Her fear of the Lachine Canal had been so great as a child that she'd sobbed and begged her parents to keep her home when her school said they were going there on a field trip. And it hadn't gotten better as an adult. With each mysterious death and missing person last seen at the water, Amélie heard her grandmother's words of caution buzzing around the back of her mind.

They built the walls high for a reason.

So the idea that Théo would suggest the canal—of all places—had been a surprise. And an unpleasant one at that. But once the leg cramps, twisted ankles from deep potholes, and pre-coffee socializing became too much, Amélie caved. While she was hesitant at first, the smooth and even pavement, flat trail, and lack of people eventually won her over. She would run through the Old Port, past the closed shops and cafes preparing to open, past the empty parks and the glass windows of popular restaurants, all the way to the benches near the edge of the water. But never past that.

She braces her hands on her knees, legs shaking, and breathes deeply, trying to catch her breath. She closes her eyes and focuses on inhaling slowly through her mouth, and expelling it slowly through her nose. Her heart hammers against her ribs, adrenaline pulsing through her veins, and when her lungs refuse to draw in enough oxygen to calm her body down, she begins to panic. Her chest is tight, iron ribs refusing to budge as her lungs try to expand and pull in air, head swimming. She counts back from ten, grabbing the bench with one hand for support as she sways. When she gets to one and finds herself none the calmer for it, she claws for the emergency inhaler in her pants' pocket.

She wraps her fingers around the blue plastic and pulls, the end of it stuck in the fabric. She tugs harder, ripping the Ventolin from her track pants and accidentally throwing it forward. It flies into the concrete wall, the metal tube of medication dislodging from the chamber, which cracks and breaks into pieces as it hits the hard surface.

Amélie tries not to panic, but she can already see white spots creeping into her line of sight, and her legs wobble like they're made of jello. Feeling like she's about to fall over, she drags herself around the back of the bench and onto the seat. She braces her elbows on her knees and hangs her head between her legs, eyes closed and mind racing.

Ten.

Nine.

In.

Eight.

Seven.

Out.

Her heart begins to slow, body and brain beginning to calm down.

In.

Six.

Five.

She inhales through her mouth, lungs filling a little more than last time.

Out.

She releases through her nose, coughing as her body relaxes and the adrenaline begins to release its hold on her.

Four.

Amélie opens her eyes and stares at her feet, looking at the small rocks and cigarette butts that litter the ground around the bench. Small cubes of green and brown glass are hidden behind one of the legs, evidence of smashed beer bottles and party nights.

Three.

In.

Two.

She looks up at the canal wall, feeling exhausted and in a fog, but able to breathe.

One.

She's drained and dreads the walk back to the apartment. Normally she'd jog back, or try to race herself again, but given the sudden asthma attack she knows its best to take it easy. She kicks herself mentally for not taking her emergency money with her, picturing the spare change in the bowl by the door that she could be using to take the metro home if she'd been smart enough to take it with her.

She sits there for what feels like hours, knowing she's going to be late for work, and eventually forces herself to stand. She's weaker than she imagined she'd be, her legs leaden, and braces herself against the wall as she falls forward. No, she doesn't look forward to the walk home at all.

Stay away from the water, Amélie.

Her hand quivers as she realizes how close she is to the edge of the canal, and she can feel herself beginning to panic again, throat getting tight and heartbeat gaining speed. She closes her eyes and tries to silence the voice in her mind that sounds like *grand maman*. She doesn't need another asthma attack. Not when she's far from home and alone by the water. What she needs is to relax, to not be afraid, to be at peace.

She opens her eyes and peeks at the canal, before closing them tight again. There's nothing there, but what else would she see? A demon rising up from the deep?

... the water ...

She opens them, slow this time, and looks out at the water as the early morning sun catches the waves and turns them from dark brown to gemstone blue in the light. Amélie lets out a breath she didn't even know she was holding, eyes focusing on the shimmering surface. The water splashes softly against the concrete and, before long, she feels almost normal. She loosens her white-knuckled grip on the railing and leans against it comfortably, enjoying the way the breeze feels on her flushed skin. She watches as seagulls swoop over the water and land in clusters, little bundles of white bobbing up and down. She looks down into the water.

A man's face looks up at hers.

She swallows a scream and shuts her eyes.

Stay away from the water, Amélie.

Shaking, she opens her eyes, hoping the man was a figment of her imagination. He wasn't. He looks up at her through the water, eyes wide in horror, mouth agape. At first, she thinks it's a body, but when she sees that the figure is moving, she realizes the man is still alive.

Alive, but drowning.

"Help! Someone! ANYONE! Please, HELP!" she screams, coughing from the effort. Her lungs aren't strong, and they wheeze objections from inside her chest. "Please! Help! HELP!"

She scans the road for anyone, but she's alone. Amélie looks down at the man in terror. He kicks and tries pulling his body through the water with his arms, but it's not enough for him to break the surface of the canal. He stares at her through the black, eyes begging for aid, movements getting slower and more lethargic as he draws in water with each desperate gulp for air.

She's seen men die before, it comes with working at a major hospital, but to watch someone drown …

Amélie grabs the railing with sweat slicked fingers and pulls herself up onto the wall, her heart in her throat.

… *the water* …

Her body doesn't want to comply with her brain, and it freezes in place when she reaches the top of the wall. She looks down into the cold water, the calm waves and melodic sound of the splashing belying the panic in both her and the man below the surface.

… *Amélie* …

She closes her eyes, heart racing and lungs heavy, and dives.

Stay away from the water, Amélie.

She propels herself down through the water, chest ready to burst and legs heavy from both the morning's workout and the fear running through her body. She's close to the man, can see him plain as day, and reaches a hand towards him. He stares at her, eyes wide, and grabs onto her. He pulls, trying to drag himself towards Amélie, but tugging her further towards him instead.

They can never go home, no matter how much they try.

Amélie kicks wildly, trying to drag the two of them towards the surface, but when the man pulls desperately at her again, they sink deeper into the canal. Her lungs burn and threaten to burst, and she knows she doesn't have long before her body forces her to draw in air. The man claws at her, desperation in his eyes, but when he only pulls her deeper for a third time Amélie pushes his hand from her arm and begins to kick herself towards the surface, alone.

A hand grabs her ankle.

She kicks out hard, trying to get free of the man, but when she looks back, she sees that it's a young woman who's taken hold this time. Like the man's, her eyes are wild and desperate, and she tries to swim to freedom above only to pull Amélie down with her.

The man is there, waiting, and he clings to Amélie's arm. She feels another hand on her, this time grabbing the hem of her shirt, and sees a child in outdated clothes holding onto her in terror. Another person, this one in a heavy winter coat, grabs her other leg and tries to pull himself up towards land, only to drag the five of them out of view from the walls of the Lachine Canal.

Another hand grabs her, fingers tangling themselves deep in her hair.

They can never go home ...

Amélie tries to scream, the sound lost in the absolute silence, and her lungs pull in freezing liquid. She coughs, but each desperate gasp for air brings in more water. She thrashes beneath the waves, kicking and biting at the hands pulling her down, veins filling with ice.

She struggles against the tide, the water feeling heavier than mud, as she claws for the surface. Things begin to move through the shadows, fingers reaching for land, eyes, wide like her own, staring back. Amélie sinks deeper into the black, watching with horror as bodies, most long forgotten, swim towards the surface and grab at her, trying to drag themselves out of the water, desperate to go home.

But they can never go home.

They built the walls high for a reason.

LITTLE BLACK BOOK

Originally published in The Women in Horror Annual, *February 2016.*

He stands at the end of the driveway, his book tucked under his arm as he fixes his starched white collar and straightens his tie. He picks a bit of lint off his beige khakis, takes a deep breath, and marches up the walkway. As he rings the bell, he catches a glimpse of himself in the glass of the screen door, and hurriedly runs a hand through his short blond hair.

The woman who answers the door is dressed comfortably in ripped jeans and a fitted white t-shirt, her long brown hair pulled back in a topknot. She rolls her eyes the second she sees who's waiting eagerly at the door.

"Hello, ma'am. Do you have a moment to spare this fine morning?"

"No. Go away."

"Please, I'll only be a—"

"Still no. Now get off my porch."

His smile flickers momentarily as he stares at her, but he puts it back in place as quickly as it faltered and tries again.

"I'll only be a minute, Lena, and if by the end of it you still aren't interested—"

"I won't be," Lena interrupts him. "You knock on my door every Sunday, and every Sunday I tell you I don't want to join. Today isn't going to be any different."

"I'm willing to make you an even better offer."

She crosses her arms over her chest, shaking her head.

"I don't care how much better you think your offer is, I'm not—"

"And I'll throw in a cash incentive," he says loudly over her.

He waits patiently for her to cave and let him in and, after a few minutes go by, her curiosity finally gets the best of her.

"How much money?"

He doesn't say anything, but stares at her expectantly. Knowing he won't answer her until they get somewhere private, she sighs and unlocks the screen door, pushing it open for him. He moves to walk inside, but she stops him, holding up a finger.

"Ten minutes. That's all you get to convince me. Ten. Minutes."

He flashes her an even bigger smile and follows her into the entranceway and down a long hall past the living room. The walls are covered in photos of Lena with another young woman. He stops and takes one off the wall.

"Is this Katie?"

Lena stops to look at the photo and nods. She takes it from him and hangs it back on the wall, making sure it lines up properly with the others. He takes another one down and Lena rolls her eyes.

"Do you need to touch all of them?"

"No … sorry. These are your parents?"

"Yes."

"Were you close with them?"

She takes the second photo from him and hangs it back on the wall without answering. She continues down the hall to the kitchen and he follows her obligingly. She points to a bar stool which rests by the cheap IKEA kitchen island, and he takes a seat.

"Coffee?" she asks, opening one of the cupboards and taking out two mismatched coffee mugs.

"Does it count as part of my ten minutes?"

"Absolutely. And it's closer to eight minutes now."

"Then no, thank you."

She puts one of the mugs back and closes the wooden door, porcelain rattling gently on the warped shelf inside. Lena begins fixing herself a drink in the chipped glass mug while the man sets his black leather book down on the countertop.

"The church—"

"It's not the church. It's you, and you *personally*, that's making this offer. I don't care about anyone else or about your collective cause."

"You know, some really great people belong to my congregation. We only take the best of the best … and the occasional politician!"

He chuckles at his own wit while she stares at him. She stirs some sugar into her coffee, watching through the side of the transparent mug as it dissolves into the nearly black liquid. She taps the spoon against the rim, then drops it into the dented sink. Cradling the mug in both hands, she leans against the stove and watches him through the small curls of steam rising out of her glass.

He frowns, running a hand through his hair, and continues with his spiel.

"We're, *I'm,* willing to offer you $1.5 million. It'll be non-taxable, untraceable, and no one will ask any questions about it."

Lena sips her coffee quietly, watching him but not saying anything.

"It's enough money that you'd be able to pay for your sister's treatment, and pay off the last of the bills your parents left you. I'm also willing to extend your time from the standard five to a full ten years."

"I don't get it," she says, putting her mug down on the counter and crossing her arms. "Why do you want me so badly?"

"You're hot right now. You're influential. We think you could be a major asset on our side."

"I'm none of those things! The work I have out is shit, everyone knows that, and I can't sell my manuscript to save my life."

"For now."

Lena looks at him, brow furrowed, until the meaning behind his words sink in. She frowns, shaking her head, and begins to pace across the kitchen.

"My book's going to be published, isn't it?"

"Yes. It'll be a bestseller, too."

"How do you know?"

"I just do," he says, with a shrug.

Lena begins to bite her nails, walking faster. Her skin looks paler in the sunlight streaming in through the kitchen windows, and she starts to perspire.

"It's a rip-off of an old story, and I'm a hack of a writer. You publish it and everyone's gonna know. You won't be able to get away with it."

The man laughs hard, wipes a tear from the corner of his eye, and quickly flashes his bright white teeth at Lena once again.

"We got Bush in for two terms. At the very least we can get your book published without anyone the wiser for it."

She stops her nervous pacing and resumes leaning against her stove. She picks her coffee back up and takes a huge gulp, wincing as the hot liquid burns her tongue.

"But let me guess," she drawls, "I have to make the deal or else nothing gets printed, Katie doesn't get cured, and I can add her funeral to the list of expenses I have to worry about. Is that right?"

She raises an eyebrow, skeptical, as the white-collared Devil shakes his head.

"No, not at all. I'm not like that, Lena. That's not how I work; it would be bad for business. Your book will still come out— as a sign of good faith—and I'm not going to kill your sister if you decide not to take the deal. I won't be able to take away her cancer, but I won't simply take her life. Besides, that's His job."

The man stands up and crosses the room until he's only a foot away from Lena. She leans back against the counter, heart pounding, as he reaches a hand towards her. He chuckles and opens the cupboard behind her head, getting himself a mug. After pouring himself a drink, he sits back down and takes a swig of the piping hot coffee.

"I didn't make your sister sick and I can't take her cancer away, but I can guarantee that she'll get better with treatment. I can promise you that you'll be there to see her get better, to see her get married, and to see her get pregnant. A full and happy life."

"Why do you need to murder me as payment?"

"You make it sound so barbaric. I'm not going to *murder* you, Lena. In a decade's time, you'll go to sleep and simply won't wake up. You won't even realize you haven't woken up; you'll just stop being."

"But *why*?"

"Because everything takes energy. The money for Katie's chemo, the money to pay your bills, the guarantee of good health in the years to come … all that energy has to come from somewhere. I'm not God, after all."

After a long pause, Lena shakes her head.

"I'll just use the money from my book to pay for my sister, and if it's not enough then I'll figure something out. She might get better without your help."

He nods, frowning slightly.

"She might. Or she might get worse. No one knows for sure."

Lena closes her eyes and rubs them with one hand. She can feel the headache forming under her skin, pounding at the grey matter of her brain and throbbing from behind her eyeballs down to the base of her skull.

"I know it's a lot to consider, but be realistic here. Your sister *is* going to die without my help. Without *your* help. So take the deal, help recruit for my church, and enjoy being the biggest thing since James Frey in the time you have left."

Lena chugs the last of her coffee and puts the cup on the counter. She opens one of the small cupboards above the stove and takes out a bottle of Irish cream. She unscrews the cap, pours it into the dirty mug, and lifts the mug to her lips.

"No!" the man shouts, his voice so thunderous that the glass window panes vibrate. He stands up so fast that he knocks the stool over.

Lena drops the cup, startled, and stares down at the liquor spilling across the counter from the shattered glass. She turns to the man, pale and trembling, only to see his face twisted with rage. The fine lines in his face are suddenly far deeper, his bright teeth yellowed and rotting with age, and his cheer and empathy replaced with something sinister and greedy. When he realizes she's watching him, the deep wrinkles seem to smooth themselves out, the brightness returns to his eyes, and a serene smile slowly works its way back onto his face.

"Sorry," he says placidly.

He moves his hand in a sweeping motion, and Lena turns to see that the mess has disappeared, a restored cup of liqueur waiting for her on the scratched countertop. She looks back at the man and sees the bar stool sitting undisturbed in its place next to the island, and she clutches at her chest.

"Being under the influence of drugs, alcohol, or intimidation nullifies the contract," he explains. "A sip is enough to make the deal non-binding. And I don't think either of us wants that, do we?"

Lena shakes her head slowly.

"Good."

"So how do we do this?"

He extends his left hand towards her.

"You just need to shake my hand, and then I'll add your name to my book."

She holds her hand close to her chest before speaking hurriedly.

"Make it $3 million and twelve years and you have a deal."

She holds out her hand and waits for him to make a decision.

"Done."

He grasps her hand tightly and she winces as his ring cuts into her skin. He releases his grip on her and she watches with fascination as the cut on her hand seals shut, leaving behind a small pink scar in its wake. She stares at the scar a moment longer before picking up her drink and hammering it back.

The man opens the book and Lena watches curiously as her blood falls off his ring and onto one of the thin, translucent pages. The blood hisses as it hits the paper and begins to swirl in a seemingly senseless pattern, finally spelling out her name in Lena's own handwriting.

As the man closes the book, Lena's eyes are drawn to another name. Her throat tightens and she can feel her pulse quickening.

"Why is her name in your book?" she asks quietly, her mouth suddenly dry. "Why is Katie's name in your book?"

He looks up at her, all traces of his good natured smile gone.

"Nothing is free, Lena. Not even your stolen bestseller. When your sister found out that she couldn't save her own life, she decided that she wanted to see you live your dream before she passed. It was very altruistic of her."

"No! You can't, please … "

"You should have seen how happy she was when she found out that you would get your book and she would get five more years with you."

Lena shakes her head, her eyes wide and red rimmed.

"Five years? But you said she was going to get better, get married, and have a kid!"

"She will get better and she will get married, but I only told you that she would get pregnant. I never promised you that she would give birth."

Lena's cup slides from between her fingers once again and crashes to the floor.

"But you gave me twelve years!"

"So use them wisely."

He picks up his book, smooths out a crease in his pants, and smiles at Lena. The smile is as cold, empty, and hollow as she feels.

"See you soon, Lena. And give your sister my best."

He places a small stack of brochures for the Church of Mammon neatly on the counter before leaving, the screen door clicking shut behind him.

He walks to the end of Lena's driveway, adjusts his tie and stiff white collar, and makes his way to her neighbor's door. He rings the bell and, after a moment, a small old woman answers.

"Hello ma'am," he says with a wide smile. "Do you have a moment to spare this fine morning?"

INFECTED

Originally published in Sanitarium Magazine no. 21, *May 2014.*

We collectively shuffle towards what they've named "the mess hall". The chain link fence clinks in the wind; our stomachs growl loud. At first I think I'm the only one who hears it, the gurgling and churning of acid and digestive fluids in an empty stomach, but the guards tighten their grips on their guns and put another foot between themselves and the fence. It's cold out, but the air feels good on my skin, cooling the sweat beading on my forehead.

The building in front of us is broken and run down. In its day it would have been beautiful; a tower made of polished glass, jutting out of the city skyline like a monument to human innovation. Now it stands before us cracked and covered in dirt. The front door has been removed from its hinges, leaving the building open and uninviting. We walk in, some slow, some eager, all ravenous. The scent of meat is strong enough to fill the yard and it draws us in. My heart hammers, nostrils flare, and I swallow the saliva pooling in my mouth.

I pass through the entrance, eyeing one of the empty places at a picnic table deep within. The room, what would have once been the lobby, looks as run down as the exterior. Most of the walls are covered in what could pass for Jackson Pollock paintings made of old blood and mud. The original gold paint, what little of it is still showing, is dull. Holes, some with the bullets still lodged inside, hide amongst the stains. The marble floor is cracked and chipped, marked by conflicts past. Where a receptionist once sat is a cage, not to keep things in, but to keep us out. The guard inside doesn't look convinced the cage can hold much back, as he taps on the chain fencing with the butt of his gun when we get too close.

I sit down, the old wood of the bench creaking under my weight. The paper plate in front of me holds a slab of meat grilled enough to feel warm but not enough to be considered rare. I pick it up, licking my dry lips, looking at the people gathered in the centre of the room. They stare at the rest of us, mortified. They're new to the pens and still hold on to hope that this is just a bad dream. I pick up the beef with my bare hands. They continue to watch, wide eyed, and I try to ignore them as I lift the slab of meat to my mouth.

One of them locks eyes with me and I stare into them.

Then I rip into the flesh, pulling it apart and crushing it between my teeth.

Thin beams of light shine out from between the cracks in the blinds, turning the tips of Philibert's straw blonde hair golden and making me smile. There hasn't been sun like this, *real* sun, in ages. There's only been the fluorescent glow of the day lamps, which hardly illuminate the smoky city, for a very long time. It makes me happy, warming me from the pit of my stomach to the tips of my fingers.

Today feels like a good day.

I stretch out in the hard bed, waking tired limbs and finding comfort in the rough sheets that scratch my skin. It's almost time to get up, I know the morning siren's going to ring any minute now, but I don't want to leave this spot. I want to spend the day looking at the sunshine from the warmth of my bed. I want to pull off the blinds and soak it all up, absorb as much as I can before it's gone again.

I push myself closer to Philibert, enjoying the warmth his body radiates in the cold room. He's hogged most of the blankets, again, and has rolled halfway onto my side of the mattress. He snores lightly, enough to keep me up when I'm trying to fall asleep but not loud enough to wake me once I'm under, and nestles into his pillow. I curl up beside him, pulling on the sheets to better cover myself against the fall cold. He opens his eyes and frowns, rolling himself over to his side of the bed again.

"Your skin's ice cold, woman," he says sleepily. "Don't rub up against me with it."

He pushes some of the blankets towards me, warm from his body heat, and I bury myself in them.

He sighs as I cuddle up to his back, tossing an arm over his side and touching his chest lazily. My hand trails slowly down, playing with the waist of his boxers, and I notice the tips of his mouth pull up in a tired smile. He sighs even louder, as the siren to wake the city wails, and interrupts the moment. He grumbles to himself as he gets out of bed, kicking the blankets off and heading to the washroom. I watch him walk, enjoying the way his muscles move under the skin of his lean frame. He crosses the small room, walking quickly on the cold scratched floor and closes the bathroom door behind him. There's the squeaking of taps then the familiar sound of water beating against the ceramic of the tub.

"Hey!" I call through the door. "It's supposed to be my turn for a shower. You had one yesterday."

He doesn't answer me, and I realize he probably can't hear me under all the water. I hop out of bed, crossing the room in a few quick strides, and open the washroom door a crack.

"Philibert, it's my turn for a shower today. What are you doing?"

"I need one."

"You had your turn yesterday..."

He doesn't say anything, just continues to soap up behind the shower doors.

"Philibert..."

"Can't you just take yours tomorrow, Tiph? I have to go to work, and I'm all sweaty from helping to rebuild the school in the East district yesterday. You have the day off, so take yours tomorrow. Okay?"

He sounds frustrated, and he does have a point. It's not like I have anywhere important to be today.

"Sure, yeah, no problem."

I close the door behind me and head down the hall to the kitchen. The walls on the way are empty, no photos hung in glass frames. Holes and scratches from nails poorly hammered adorn them instead, the memories safe in our heads and the paper saved for something more useful. Only a finger painting, Philibert's name and mine in a lopsided heart, hints to some kind of life inside this unit. I walk into the kitchen, stomach growling, and search for something to eat.

The floor is covered in all different tiles, a mosaic of anything that would fit and stick to the ground. The counters are old and stained by older food that wasn't able to be fully washed off. The doors are off two of the cupboards, and the wooden door of the pantry doesn't match. I like how it looks, a patchwork kitchen, and how it reminds me of the quilts my mother used to make for me growing up. Bits and pieces of everything around me, all stuck together to make something new.

I pull a box of cereal from the shelf then measure a perfect cup, dumping it into a chipped orange bowl. The cereal is brown and looks like something I may have fed my guinea pig when it was still alive. I then pour a measured cup of powdered milk into the bowl, mix it with a metal spoon, and dig in. Despite the bitter taste it leaves in my mouth, it fills my stomach and meets the minimum requirements for nutritional value.

Once I'm done, I put the bowl in the sink next to the dirty dishes from last night's supper, and head back to the bedroom to get changed. Philibert's nearly done dressing, the brown pants and navy top fresh from the laundry complex. The shirt is too loose on him and the pants are too tight, but there's nothing he can do except hope that the next batch of uniforms fit better. They wash all the soiled uniforms to-

gether, and deliver clean ones once a week. All the sizes are standard-
ized, and even though he's a medium, the uniforms never fit him like
they should.

"What are your plans for lunch?" I ask, pulling my civilian clothes
out from the bottom drawer of the dresser.

"The same as always. Why?"

"Well I was thinking, maybe we could go over to Sarah's for lunch?
We haven't seen her in a while, and I know she has the day off... plus
her kids will be at school."

He pulls the shirt tight, making sure it's neatly tucked into his
pants, then runs his fingers over the collar to check it's properly
folded.

"I mean, if you have too much work to do, that's fine. I'll go alone
or maybe we can see her tonight..."

"No, no, that should be fine," he says quickly, picking his card key
off the nightstand and slipping it into his breast pocket. The second
siren wails, telling the city the work day is about to begin. He crosses
the room and kisses me quickly on the lips before rushing off down
the hall. Fabric rustles, followed by a zipper sliding closed.

"Love you!" I call, hoping he heard me over the loud slam of the
door.

I head to the washroom and run a cloth under the warm water, careful to use only what I need. Once the hot water tank is empty, it stays
empty until the end of the week. I still need a shower tomorrow and
dishes still need to get done. I wash myself down and rinse the rag out,
leaving it to dry on the edge of the sink. I quickly brush my teeth and

try to comb out my long brown waves, eager to spend as much time in the sun as I can before the night comes. The plastic teeth pull painfully at the knots in my hair, making me grimace. I put the comb on the bathroom shelf, tie my locks back in a ponytail, and hurriedly pull my clothes on. The grey pants and t-shirt wash out my already pale skin, but at least they fit me properly. I sit on the edge of the bed and pull on my socks. A beam of light falls across my face, making me smile.

I wipe my mouth with the back of my hand. The cow's blood stains my skin red but camouflages into my crimson jumper. My stomach is full, but I'm still hungry. I eye the paper plate belonging to the man sitting next to me, and clench my jaw. I look away, staring at the ceiling, and run my hand through my hair absentmindedly. Long brown strands come out, sticking to my dirty fingers, and my breath catches in my throat. I rub my palm against my thigh, some of my brown hair sticking to my uniform and the rest falling onto the ground. My hands begin to quiver, so I interlace my fingers and place them in my lap, trying to think about anything other than the slab of half-eaten meat next to me or how my body is beginning to shut down.

I must look like Martha did when I saw her last; her curly black hair falling out like a cancer patient in chemo, dark circles under her eyes, jaundice creeping into her olive skin. It was only a few days ago they moved her to Pen B. I wonder if she ever saw her boyfriend again, or if he recognized her through his fever. I wonder if Philibert will know me when he sees me again, if he'll cry at my patchy scalp and blueing nails. I look at the plastic wedding ring he gave me and I hope they let him have it back after I'm dead; I don't want them to burn it like they do everything else.

"Get off!" someone screams.

It's the girl who watched me eat, the girl who couldn't look away. She can't be older than twelve, maybe thirteen. Her scraggly hair is in two braids and, unlike the rest of us, she looks good in red. Her skin hasn't yellowed enough to look harsh in the clothes they've given us, and if it wasn't for the fevered look in those brown eyes I'd have thought she was healthy.

A man is hanging on to her arm, saliva dripping from his open mouth on to the marble floor. He pulls her close, the only evidence of the meal that was on his plate a red stain on the white paper. She pulls away from him hard, straining against him, her shoulder wrenched nearly out of its socket as she tries to get away. We all watch, but none of us move to help her. I don't know if it's from apathy or shock, but not one of us come to her aid as the man throws himself at her, teeth digging into her upper arm.

The guards begin to shout instructions to us and at each other. The one in the cage radios to his colleagues that there's a "situation" in the mess hall. They begin ushering us out of the room, forcing us back the way we came. Everyone around me gets up and shambles towards the door. One of the guards fires his gun into the ceiling, spraying us with dust and plaster, bellowing for us to get a move on.

I stay seated and watch the girl, the human in me unable to look away and the monster I'm becoming not wanting to. She's screaming for me to do something, looking at me with pleading wild eyes. She kicks out, flailing, as the man takes another bite of her arm. He tries to better position himself on top of her, the rubber of his shoe slipping on the wet floor. He pins her down and rips into her throat, pulling away with a mouthful of skin and stringy muscle. She slowly stops fighting, her head turned towards me as she dies.

The room is nearly empty of people when I finally get up and make my way to the doors. More guards enter the room from a staircase in the back, one of them carrying two large black bags. I turn away from them and begin pushing past the last few people, trying to get out of the hall faster now. Their boots thud heavily against the floor, and it reminds me of the beating of a war drum.

Then they stop as suddenly as they started. Two shots are fired fast, then after a moment a third rings out. I stop moving and look over my shoulder. The man is unrecognizable, dead atop the little girl. Even though her head is turned away, gazed fixed on where I sat, I can feel her eyes watching me.

As I move into the yard, I realize the answer to my question is no.

How can I expect Philibert to recognize me, when even I don't?

The city used to be so beautiful in the fall. The leaves on the trees turning orange and red, squirrels running over lawns in search of food for the winter, the air cool enough for a coat but warm enough for a walk.

Now everything's cold and grey. Grey and brown really; dry grass, earth and ash. Gardens are empty and starved of water. Dirt and dust coats the buildings, so heavily in places that it's hard to remember them without tinted windows. I walk carefully, planning out each step before I take it. There isn't much in the way of rubble to trip on, most of it having been collected and taken away to the waste pile. They try to reuse or recycle as much as they can from the demolished homes, but whatever can't be given new life sits in the massive garbage heap. The small stones and cracks are what threaten to twist my ankles as I walk. But those always used to trip me up, when I'd wear stilettos and pants a size too tight.

I smile, enjoying the memories of high heels and days gone by.

I roll the sleeves of my jacket up, wanting to keep from the cold but also wanting to feel sun on my skin for the first time in weeks. When the bombs went off, we couldn't see the sun for months. Then, slowly, we began to see the shape of the sun from behind the clouds of smoke and dust. Now it's starting to peek out from behind the smog, but we all know it's going to be a long time before the air is clear enough for it to light up the city like it once did. Until then, we'll live behind the daytime fluorescents that flicker and buzz like fireflies.

I walk through the city districts, careful to keep to the sidewalks as trucks full of guards and supplies speed by. Their wheels kick up dust and make my eyes sting. I weave my way through the maze of streets and city districts. A black truck with a neon yellow biohazard sign rushes by, and I hold my breath. Inside, it carries the diseased and the dying. It transports the last of the plague out of the city, keeping the rest of us safe from the infection that decimated the population over eight years ago. I watch it speed down the road, taking a sharp turn out of sight. I exhale loud and roll my shoulders, trying to work out the sudden tension before continuing my walk.

I turn off the main road that runs through the two largest districts, and begin to roam what would've once been a quiet niche of the city. The rich families used to live here. They'd spend money on overpriced homes designed to look like suburban townhouses, while enjoying the luxuries only living in the heart of a metropolis could bring. It's eerily quiet, almost silent, like I'm the only one in the world left. As I walk further, the air gets thicker and full of ash. Then I hear a crackling on the wind and what sounds like screaming, and I follow it to its source.

One of the houses is being burned to the ground. A group of men stand in front of the home, draped in protective gear and armed with flamethrowers. Two fire trucks are parked close by, hoses ready and waiting should the fire get out of hand. I move closer, wanting to get a better view of the flames. The air is warm from the blaze and my hair sticks to the sweat on my skin. As I cross the strip of road to the yard, a gust of wind pushes a cloud of ash into me. The tiny particles force their way past my nostrils and into my lungs. I double over, coughing hard, my throat burning and eyes watering.

"Ma'am," someone calls.

I look up to see a member of the Patrol approaching. The gas mask he wears muffles his voice, and he moves towards me fast with his hand on the holster of his gun.

"Are you alright ma'am?" he asks slowly.

"Yes, yes," I sputter through coughs. "Ash... breathe..."

The guard removes his hand from his gun and signals for two guards I hadn't noticed to stand down.

"Ma'am, I'm sorry, but you're not allowed to be this close. If you could just stand further back, please."

I nod and step away from him. I spit on the pavement next to me and cough again, this time to try and clear my throat.

"Why aren't you putting the fire out?" I ask, voice rough.

He looks back at the house, not meeting my gaze.

"We found... signs... of possible contamination with infectious materials. As per standard protocol, we're eliminating all traces of the biohazard. Now, ma'am , if you'd kindly step ba—"

"I heard screaming," I cut him off.

He stands straighter, looking me in the eye this time, before answering.

"You must be mistaken. Now, ma'am, I won't ask you again to stand back."

I nod and move to the other side of the road, hand on my chest as I watch the fire burn.

I throw up in the corner of the yard, but no one cares. Not even the guards who will have to clean it. Stomach acid and everything I've eaten in the last day hits the ground, mixing with the dirt and grass. Some of it splashes onto my uniform and shoes. My stomach churns, hungry for the food I've just given up. I lean against the fence and bend over, letting my head hang. The liquefied contents of my stomach slowly fill the cracks and craters of the ground, pooling around the solid chunks.

None of the sick men and women roaming around the yard notice me. None of them seem upset by the incident in the mess hall, like they've seen this a hundred times before.

Maybe they have.

I slump to the ground, sweat beading down my face, and unzip the top of my crimson one-piece. The air on my chest feels good, but not enough to cool me down. I unzip the uniform even more, exposing me from the sides of my breasts to my navel. I want to rip the clothing off, to walk through the pen naked. Even though the fabric is thin, it feels as warm as a parka with the blazing fever. I lick my lips, realizing how dry they are and how dry my cracked, yellow, skin is.

The wind ruffles my hair. I take a fistful in my hand and pull slowly, testing its strength. My scalp releases the strands, giving up the brown locks Philibert used to play with. Not all of them come out, some of them clinging to my head. I pull harder, ripping them out. With both hands, I pull, tearing all I can out from the roots. It doesn't hurt like I know it should.

I slip my right arm out from my uniform, then my left. I let the top of the one-piece hang limp on the ground around me, and pull my legs up to my chest in an attempt to fake modesty and get comfortable. I lie back against the cold metal fence, close my eyes and try to sleep.

Approaching the door, I pull a card key from my back pocket, worried for just a second that it may have fallen out on the jog over, and hand it to the guard stationed out front. He frowns at me, and swipes the card with his handheld reader. It beeps twice, giving me clearance to the building's inner entrance.

The heavy steel doors open and I walk through. Another officer waits inside, and a woman in scrubs sits behind a reception desk.

"Good afternoon," she says with a bored smile. "How may I help you today?"

"I'm here to see Philibert Cabral. He works upstairs in—"

"Data analysis," she finishes for me.

I nod as she continues.

"I'm just going to need some information, if that's alright?" she asks, opening a binder lined with sign in sheets. She flips to an empty one and waits for me to answer.

I nod again, knowing to refuse is to be escorted out.

"Your name, please."

"Tiphany Cabral."

"Relation?"

"Wife."

"Date of your most recent vaccination?"

"September Seventeenth, 2018. So, yesterday."

"Wonderful. And, last one, do you have a checkpoint paper from today?"

"No, sorry."

She jots something down and opens one of the desk drawers, taking out a glass vial with a cotton swab sealed inside. She reaches into a box on her desk, pulling out a pair of plastic gloves and putting them on.

"No problem. I'm just going to need to take a cheek swab to make sure you're clean, and then you'll be issued a checkpoint paper that will give you clearance to public buildings for the next three hours. After that, you'll be required to submit to another swab."

"No problem."

The receptionist/nurse picks up the vial with the swab and she approaches me. She uncaps the tube and I open my mouth, noticing that the guard has moved closer to me. I wait for her to finish scratching me with the cotton tip, trying not to gag when she puts it in too far. She puts the swab back in the glass and walks back to her desk.

Behind it is a counter, government issued, cluttered with test-tube racks, labels, a few bottles of blue liquid and a disposal unit for hazardous materials. She slides the vial in a holder and pours some of the blue liquid into it, filling just enough to cover the cotton end of the swab. I cross my arms, always annoyed during this procedure; I've had my shots kept up to date and there's no reason for me to need testing. I know what the outcome is going to be, it's always—

"I'm sorry Mrs. Cabral, but your test results are showing up purple, indicating a trace of infection," she says slowly.

It takes me a moment to decipher her words and once I do, it takes me even longer to figure out how to react to them.

"Excuse me?"

"Your results have turned up positive for potential infection."

"But it's blue."

"No, ma'am, that's purple," she insists, showing me the tube as proof.

"I don't mean *that's* blue. I mean my results are always blue. Always."

I can feel sweat on the back of my neck and my hands are unsteady. The room tilts a bit to the left and I wonder if I should brace myself against a wall to keep from falling. It's a mistake. It has to be. She probably poured the wrong liquid in. All the blue solutions are unmarked, so how's she supposed to tell the right one apart from the rest?

"Yes, but because of th—"

"I'm not infected. I'm clearly not rabid," I tell her, matter-of-factly.

I can hear the guard muttering under his breath and from the corner of my eye I realize he's holding a walkie. His free hand is resting on the stun-gun in his holster, his eyes fixed on me.

"Please, ma'am, if you'd just relax a moment and take a deep breath. These in-house results are never conclusive. They only show that you have bacteria in your blood similar to that of the disease which, in your case, could be the result of a fresh inoculation," she tells me, in a soothing voice.

"So then what's the problem? If you know it's from my shot, just let me in," I try and reason, drumming my fingers restlessly against my thigh.

"As I'm sure you're aware, standard procedure is that we isolate the source of potential infection, have a full medical exam administered, and upon a clean bill of health you'll be released."

"Released? So I'm a prisoner now?" I ask, throat much too tight.

"A patient if you're sick, and an inconvenienced citizen if you're not. It's just a precaution to ensure public safety, ma'am. If you'd just follow Clay, he'll escort you to a waiting area until the proper transport arrives."

"Alone? What about Philibert? He's going to wonder where I am. He'll be worried. He'll want to know what's being done."

"We'll inform him immediately and he'll be brought down to the holding bay to accompany you to the appropriate facility. If you'd just please follow Clay..."

The guard comes up beside me, his hand now resting directly on the stun gun, and leads me to a side door I hadn't noticed before. Of course there'd be a side door; if I was rabid, they wouldn't want me back on the streets to become a roamer, but they wouldn't want me in the building either. He slides a card key in the reader and it gives a shrill beep before the lock releases. He pushes the thick steel door open to reveal a sitting room that could've come from an old IKEA catalogue.

Crisp white walls, squishy sofas, and some chairs that look more like art than they do comfortable, all circle a long white coffee table stacked with books. The door clangs shut behind me, and I spin on my heel. The guard has sealed me in, alone, and I take a seat on one of the couches. From this angle, a thin gap between the curtains is visible and I notice a strip of silver.

Another door.

My heart's pounding so hard that I think my ribs are rattling. I fold my arms across my chest and cross my left leg over my right. I can't have the infection. I *can't* because I just took my shots. The vaccine keeps the virus away, keeps us from going rabid, from turning cannibal, from the devastation the world survived.

But what if I'm sick?

But I'm not.

Why is this room so warm?

I wait for what feels like years until I hear the now-familiar sound of a lock unlocking. I look over my shoulder at the door and see my husband, escorted by the less than pleasant guard.

"Philibert!" I say his name like it's the most beautiful word I've ever said. I stand up quickly and turn towards him.

He takes a step away from me, like something's pushed him back. His gaze darts around the room quickly, constantly shifting from me to his surroundings. The guard raises his hand, palm towards me and hand open.

"Ma'am, I'm going to have to ask you to stay back."

"Seriously?"

"Protocol."

I stare at the guard, my eyes stinging, and I try not to look as upset as I feel. None of us speak for a moment. The Philibert gives me a big smile, his lips stretched too tight and too wide, trying to diffuse the tension.

"Hey, Tiph," he says, much too gently. "How're you feeling?"

"Fine. I'm feeling perfectly fine and this is all bullshit. You *have* to know that. Please tell me you know that."

"Of course, babe. Of course it is and we're going to get all of this straightened out, I promise."

I raise my eyebrow and shake my head, looking anywhere but at him.

"You've never, in your life, called me 'babe' so don't start now. Don't try to fucking pacify me with a pet name, okay?" I say, loudly.

The guard moves forward, ready to jump between us should I suddenly spring forward and attack.

"I'm sorry," I say, taking a step back. "I'm just really stressed, ok?"

"Yeah, Tiph, I know. But you're going to be fine. The transport is going to be here soon, they'll run a few tests, ask you a few questions and I'll meet you there in a couple hours," he tells me, stepping out from behind the guard.

"Meet me there? Aren't you coming with me?"

Philibert clears his throat and straightens his shirt before answering. His face seems flushed and he won't meet my gaze.

"They need me to answer a few questions about you, to help them retrace your steps. What you do, who you've been with the last twenty-four hours, that kind of stuff. The second they're done, I'll head right over."

"Why would they ask *you* where I've been? You've been here all day, it's not like you're going to know. And who I've been with? Sexually? Just you, and you know that."

He shifts his weight from foot to foot.

"Tiph, I know, but that's what they want, so I'm going to be as helpful as I can. Anything to help you get better is my priori—"

"I'm not sick!"

The guard points the stun gun directly at my chest.

"I know. I know you're not, Tiph. We'll get this all sorted and you'll be out in no time. Promise."

Philibert walks away from me and heads to the door. The guard backs up, not turning his back to me, and swipes his card key in the reader. The door opens with another beep.

"I'll see you in a bit, Tiph," Philibert says as he steps through to the other side.

The guard follows him through, gun still raised, and shuts the door behind them.

I wake up in a room, as naked as I feel. No single piece of furniture adorns the small quarters. The light fixtures are flat and too high for me to reach, and there's no doorknob where the door is. Three of the walls are white and, like everything else in these pens, show signs of a struggle. Old stains peak out from under hasty paint jobs. Scratches cover the floor and dig deep into the plaster on the walls. The fourth wall is made of glass, and I see another room like this one on the other side.

I'm curled in the fetal position, my crimson jumper replaced by a white hospital gown, my wedding band still on my finger. For the first time since being infected, I don't feel warm. My skin isn't hot or too tight on my body. I feel healthy again. I feel better. I push myself into a sitting position and smile as the wood underneath me feels cold. *Cold.* I run my hands over my scalp and the skin is smooth and soft. I inspect my arms, my legs, and I even pull my gown up to run my hands over my chest. The scars and marks that littered my body are gone.

I feel like me again.

In the other room the door opens and Philibert walks in.

"Mrs. Cabral?" a man asks from the door behind the drapes, pushing them aside with his clipboard.

"Yes," I seethe from my spot on the sofa.

As though there's anyone else in here.

"If you'd kindly bring all your personal belongings and follow me."

He leads me through a narrow tunnel to an alleyway. A black truck bearing the yellow biohazard sign is parked and waiting. I stop dead in my tracks, not wanting to get a step closer to the vehicle. The guard looks at me and waits patiently for me to continue onwards. I swallow hard and keep moving. It's just a mix up and I need to be brave. No, not brave; complacent. I've had my vaccination and there's no need to be brave when I'm immune.

Inside are seats fastened to the walls with harnesses to keep people secured. Two of the seats are already occupied. One of them is a woman, late fifties, who looks as frightened as I feel. She looks at me and recoils, shrinking back in her chair. The other one, a boy in his late teens, doesn't seem to understand what's happening, and his eyes look wide and unfocused. His skin's pale, yellowing in patches, and I know he'll be rabid soon.

He looks like every poster for the disease that I'd ever seen; warning us to report any and all roamers, listing the signs of infection beside the photo of someone who used to be human. Fever, bloodshot eyes, yellowing skin, incoherent speech, sexual aggression, violent outbursts, rage and hunger. Philibert used to say the rabid want only the three animal Fs; to feed, fuck, and fight.

The man mutters something, trying to lean forward. He's watching me now, and his eyes are void of intelligent thought.

"I'm not getting in this thing with *him* in here," I tell the officer, eyes fixed on the boy.

"Ma'am, the harnesses will keep him restrained, and I'll put you next to the woman on the opposite wall. I promise you, we take security measures to prevent patients from getting free. Now, if you'll just take a seat," he tells me, pointing to a chair near the old woman.

I climb the steps of the truck and sit. The officer ties me in and I feel like a prisoner. Each hand is fastened to the opposite shoulder, my legs are strapped to the floor of the truck, and my body is secured in a harness that looks more like a straitjacket than anything close to a seatbelt. The journey to the medical centre is a long one. It's at least an hour's drive away and isolated from the city.

Along the way, we pick up more people. Two middle aged men, both yellow around the edges, and a woman who can't be much older than I am. She's harnessed in next to me. She doesn't seem sick, but doesn't seem worried either.

"I'd shake your hand if I had one free," she jokes.

I can't help but chuckle, even if it feels a bit strange for me to be laughing at a time like this.

"Martha," she says, winking.

"Tiphany Cabral."

She gives me a once over, frowning.

"You look too young to be a wife."

"What?"

She nods to my left hand, where a plastic ring from a costume shop rests around my finger.

"Either you put that on the wrong hand this morning, or your husband made do with what he had."

I close my eyes and smile, nodding to her. "You know how it was; people thought the end was nigh and figured it was their last chance to get hitched. Suddenly standards didn't matter and people took what they could get," I explain.

"You seem happy about settling, though."

"I am. Well, I didn't really settle, but I probably wouldn't have gotten married to him at sixteen either," I admit.

Martha nods, understanding. She looks around the truck and hums to herself. She's comfortable here, at ease, and her courage makes me strong.

Philibert walks close to the glass partition, watching me. He hasn't shaven in a while, the stubble on his chin longer than it was when we last spoke. He's in his grey civilian uniform, but the shirt looks wrinkled and dirty. He puts a hand against the glass and smiles at me, eyes dull.

I put my hand on the glass and smile back, leaning my head on the window.

He pulls away for a moment, before putting his hand back and leaning in close.

"Why do you look so upset? I mean, I know you weren't expecting me to be bald, *I* wasn't expecting me to go bald, but I'm better."

My voice catches in my throat and I feel my eyes sting as the words hang in the air.

"I'm better," I whisper this time.

I try and relax into my chair, but the straps pull uncomfortably on my chest. I wiggle in them, huffing and puffing. With all the people, and the harness around me, it's hot in the truck.

"Ugh, these straps are biting into my skin; I think they're cutting off my circulation. Hey," I shout, in hopes someone will hear me, "can you loosen these, please? It's too tight."

No one from the front cabin of the truck answers so I call even louder.

Nothing.

"I think they're used to hearing people yell. It's probably why they aren't answering," Martha tells me.

I frown, but know she's right.

"So, how'd you end up here? Get bitten by a roamer?" she asks casually, like two friends talking over a drink at a bar.

"Oh, I'm not sick," I tell her quickly, "this is just a mistake."

"Of course."

"No, really. I had my shot yesterday, so my test showed signs of possible infection. I'm not actually rabid," I laugh. "And you? Did they screw up your vaccine too?"

"Oh, no. I'm definitely infected."

"What?" I ask, unsure I heard her properly.

"I'm infected."

"How? I mean, you can't be sure. Everyone's been given shots, the antivirus. I mean, it could just be a mist—"

"My boyfriend came home from the plant last night. A roamer had attacked him and bit one of his fingers off. The vaccines can only do so much, you know? So we knew he was done for. A dead man walking kind of thing," she tells me in a matter of fact tone. "Anyways, we wait the night, hoping that maybe he'll be able to fight off the infection. He wasn't. He started turning around breakfast. I don't want to be here without him, and I don't want him dying alone and afraid. So I slept with him for the last time."

"You what?" I ask horrified.

"Slept with him," she says calmly. "They came and got him early this afternoon, while I was out. When I got home and he wasn't there, I called them to come collect me."

"You're insane!"

"No, no. It's brilliant. This way we'll be in the pens together. We'll both turn and won't be alone."

"You're fucking crazy," I hiss, pulling as far away from her as I can.

I'd heard rumours of suicide by roamer, but never believed them. Who would choose this for themselves? What was she thinking? The teen across from us begins wailing, beating the back of his head against the truck wall.

"Crazy? Crazy would have been to go on without him, to keep on fighting. Giving in is the sanest thing we can do."

He looks like he hasn't slept in a very long time. There's a knocking, and then the door to Philibert's room opens a crack.

"Sir, my name is Dr. Stephenson. I've been charting your wife's condition since her admission to the facility. May I come in? It's important I speak with you."

Philibert nods. The door opens to grant access to a man in a white lab coat. Under it he wears the regulated purple uniform of a healthcare worker and carries a clear plastic clipboard. He watches me, expression blank, and flips to a page in his notes. I pull myself off the window and smile to the doctor.

"It's nice to finally meet you. They told me a physician was assigned to me, but they never said who."

"How did she contract it?" Philibert asks bluntly.

The doctor looks back down at his paper, jots something down, and turns his attention to Philibert.

"She told the admissions nurse she'd accidentally inhaled fresh ash at the scene of a decontamination fire. She hadn't been wearing a protective mask and likely ingested biohazardous material." After a moment of silence passes between them, the doctor continues. "We need to discuss her options."

Philibert doesn't bother looking up, but rather he continues to stare at me. He furrows his brow and exhales deeply, his warm breath leaving a mark on the glass.

"What options?" I ask, my attention now on the doctor.

"I know it's difficult to talk about, Mr. Cabral, but it's important that we know what to do during this final stage."

"What final stage?" I ask.

When both are silent, I knock on the glass. Both of them take a step back from the window and Philibert looks unsettled.

"As you've been explained, those infected have a terminal prognosis. Tiphany is degenerating steadily, and if she continues at this rate she'll, regrettably, pass on within the week."

"What the hell do you mean by 'pass on'? I'm fine!" I shout, banging my open hand against the window.

"Right now, her brain is shutting down. She's lost the proper function of her kidneys and liver, her respiratory rate is much too high and her pulse much too low. She's losing circulation in her extremities, as you can see by her blue fingers and toes," the doctor lies.

I look at my body, my skin pink and healthy, my fingers intact and nails well groomed.

Why is he lying to Philibert?

I'm healthy, I'm cured, and I just want to go home.

"From what we're able to tell," he continues, "she's also lost the ability to reason. Two guards found her huddled in the yard, naked, and ripping out her hair. Lu—"

"Liar! It fell out! My hair, it fell out! Stop it!" I shout, slapping my hands against the glass, "Phil, can't you see he's lying?"

Why can't they hear me?

"—ckily they were able to tranquilize her and bring her here without the use of excessive force. We had to shave her head for her own protection and we've done the best we can with her self-inflicted wounds. As you can see, she's unable to communicate using language and we don't believe she's able to understand it either."

Philibert turns away from me.

"What can you do?"

"We can either keep her isolated like she is and let the infection take its course or..."

"Or?" Philibert and I ask in unison.

"Or there's always euthanasia."

Philibert's shoulders tense and he folds his arms over his chest.

"The hell there is," I yell.

"I know it isn't what you want to hear," the doctor says in a soothing tone, "but there's nothing else we can do for her. It's the humane option for those in her state. It's quick, painless, and allows those infected to keep their integrity."

The hairs stand up on the back of my neck.

"If you need some time to think about it, I can always come back later... I understand this isn't an easy decision."

The doctor clicks his pen, retracting the ballpoint back into the plastic shaft and slipping it into his breast pocket. He pulls a walkie from his lab coat with his free hand and presses down on a button, bringing it close to his mouth to speak.

"No, wait," Philibert cuts in. His voice is thick and he looks back at me, not bothering to fake a smile. "I... I don't want her to suffer like this. You're sure she won't feel anything?" he asks.

"No! No!" I yell, beating my fists against the glass, willing the window to break.

This can't be happening. I'm fine, I'm fine!

"Just the prick of a needle, like a booster shot or a vaccine."

The truck bounces up and down as we drive over what can only be a gravel driveway. I shout for them to get me out of here, that there's a mistake. Don't they know there's a mistake? I'm not like the others, I'm not sick. I'm not insane. I'm not rabid. Can't they see that?

"If your husband was sick," she says, over the boy's screaming, "if your husband was dying, what would you have done?"

There's a sickening crunch and a gurgling sound that follows. The teen has cracked his head open against the wall, blood dripping onto the floor below him. Yet still, he thwacks his head against the truck, beating his brains in, shouting, until he's finally quiet.

The truck comes to a halt. The back doors squeal in protest as the guards open them. Sounds of men talking, people screaming, a gun firing all rush in and greet us.

We're finally at the pens.

I wake up to bright lights and the smell of disinfectant. My eyes sting and my throat feels like it's been rubbed down with sandpaper. My head hurts and the room is spinning. They've wheeled a gurney into the white room and tied me to it. I turn my head towards the glass wall and see Philibert watching me. There are crow's feet where smooth skin used to be. His straw coloured hair looks like dry grass and his bright eyes are dark.

Two men enter my room. One's carrying a sheet and the other, the doctor, a syringe.

"How'd this one contract it?" the orderly asks.

"She was recently vaccinated with batch nineteen," the doctor explains, as he pricks my skin with the tip of the needle and shoots fire up my arm.

In the other room, a man walks in and gives Philibert a small brown envelope. He turns the package open and my wedding band slides into his open hand. He looks at me one last time before turning away, not wanting to watch me die. He walks to the door and pushes it open.

"If they're not careful," the orderly mumbles, "they're going to have another outbreak on their hands."

I feel tired, groggy. It's getting harder to hear them and the lights seem brighter, making my eyes hurt.

"I know. She's the seventh subject that's been brought in post-inoculation. But at least we know this test batch was a failure."

I watch the door shut behind Philibert and I close my eyes.

Centre Ice

Originally published in Canadian Dreadful, *June 2019.*

The bell rings and Jérôme approaches the counter, and the old woman standing in front of it, with a smile. Her hair tumbles around her face in thinning grey waves, shockingly long for a woman of her age. A woman with an eclectic style, she sports a worn sheepskin coat with elastic-waisted jeans and poinsettia-red galoshes, which lead a trail of rainwater from her spot at the counter to the front door.

"Mme. Elodi, you're out late. How's the rain?" the young man asks, looking past her to the plaque hanging in the foyer of the arena.

"Wet, mostly," she jokes, smiling as she leans against the wooden countertop. "It's come down hard enough that the blueberry fields are practically swimming, but thankfully the season for them is almost over."

He nods in silent agreement, but when he doesn't say anything back she sighs and offers more.

"It's not good, but I've seen worse. It rained so hard in '88 that the library roof caved in and ruined the entire reference section. But to-night isn't nearly as bad as it was then. Besides, the rain shouldn't be what's on your mind. Not with it being your last day here!"

"It's not," he says, good cheer returning to his face. "I'm going to be working through the fall again."

Jérôme smiles, unable to hide his enthusiasm at the thought of working with *Les Sangliers* for another season. Unlike the kids who worked the snack bar before him, he didn't have any plans to move, visit family, or attend another school come the end of the summer. Although he'd considered sending applications out to the bigger rinks in Québec—or even one in the neighbouring Saguenay-Lac-Saint-Jean townships—for the upcoming season, his chances of getting selected will be even better with two years experience at the rink, so Jérôme is eager to continue being the town's favourite go-to snack man for the foreseeable future.

"Very good! Édouard must be thrilled."

Jérôme shrugs, not wanting to confess that she's dead wrong. Saying his father wasn't happy about his job at the rink is an understatement, but it's an argument he's long since given up on.

"Now," the woman says, pulling him from his thoughts and a fiver from her purse, "would you be so kind as to get me a box of chocolate raisins?"

"Of course!"

He passes her the box, takes her five-dollar bill, and gives her the change.

"How's work been treating you here, dear?" she asks, tossing a toonie in the plastic tip jar.

"Good! I'm excited to start school tomorrow, although I hope I get an easy English teacher who doesn't give me too much homework. I don't want to be stuck reading books I don't care about when I could be spending time here."

"You enjoy being at the arena?"

"Love it. Sometimes, I don't want to leave."

"You sound just like your uncle."

"I wouldn't know. I guess you knew him?" he asks, eyes wandering to the entrance of the building once more.

"We go way back, yes."

She gives him a small smile and looks at her watch. Satisfied that he's no longer worrying about the rain, it's clear she's no longer interested in the conversation.

She begins to shuffle towards the doors of the stadium.

"Sorry, Mme. Elodie, but may I ask what you're doing here? The arena is about to close."

"The arena is open late tonight, sweetie. Didn't Maxime tell you? There's a town meeting after closing hours today."

"Oh, uh, I guess he forgot to mention it. Why aren't you using the town hall to meet, if you don't mind me asking?"

"Have you ever been in the old building?"

Jérôme shakes his head.

"You're lucky then. It's like the walls suck out any sunshine, even when the windows are open, and the lights buzz like flies in their sockets. If you listen closely at night, you can hear bats fluttering in the attic and the ground shifting beneath the building. It's only a matter of time before that old thing comes crashing down. I don't intend to be trapped inside it when it finally does. Do you?"

"No way. No ma'am."

She winks at him and enters the seating area as a few more elderly people walk through the front doors, through the lobby, and past his concessions counter, following Mme. Elodie into the rink.

"Jérôme, could you clean the plaque please?" his boss calls from the door of his office, only a few feet away.

"Sure thing!"

He puts a small plastic sign on the counter—BACK IN 5—and grabs a small bottle of all purpose spray and a rag before making his way to the arena's entrance.

He stares at the sign on the wall, bright gold mounted on rich mahogany, and runs a bare hand over the name on display.

Théo Brodeur.

His uncle.

He squirts some of the light pink liquid onto the sign and rubs the cleanser into the wood and metal, removing whatever dust and grime has collected on the plaque since he polished it the night before. He knows the outline of the words well, having felt them under his fingers every night since starting at the arena. Cleaning the sign has become such an easy task that he lets his eyes wander to the bust of his uncle, locked safely with his ashes behind glass in the arena wall.

A lifetime ago his dad's older brother, Théo, had singlehandedly broken the local team's twenty-seven-year losing streak, much to the town's amazement. He brought home trophies the villagers of Sainte-Élisabeth-de-Proulx had only ever prayed for in hushed voices, and he put *Les Sangliers* back on the map for junior hockey. Everyone thought he was going to make it big, and he would have, had he not been one of the victims of a landslide that had killed eight people in '67. While his life had been cut tragically short, the luck (and winning streak) Théo had brought *Les Sangliers* lived on.

He gives the plaque one last pass before returning to his post at the counter, and soon the pillars of his community begin to saunter in— his principal, the town mayor, the chief librarian—followed by some of the farming community. The door to the arena opens again, but this time his father is the one slumping towards the stadium doors, eyes glued to the heels of the people ahead of him.

"Dad!" Jérôme shouts in surprise.

The man freezes in his tracks, stopping so suddenly that the woman behind him only narrowly avoids crashing into his back. Instead of an angry huff or disparaging look, she pats him on the back and continues into the arena behind the long line of people.

"Dad?"

Édouard drags his feet to the counter, his dirty work boots leaving scuff marks and mud on the tiled floor behind him. He plays with the drawstrings that hang from the front of his coat, not looking to meet his son's smile. His Gainsborough hair, what little there is left, is matted against his forehead, and his plaid shirt is misbuttoned. Although he's never been known for being a sharp dresser, it's unusual for Édouard to look so bedraggled in public.

"Dad, what are you doing here? You never care about this kind of stuff."

His father nods, but doesn't say anything.

Jérôme leans against the edge of the counter, brushing imaginary dirt from the clean service window.

"Why did you come out this time? It's raining … "

He grunts in reply, running a sweaty palm across the front of his jacket to dry his skin, shifting his weight from foot to foot. He's quiet, and the unusual silence concerns Jérôme.

"Dad, is everything okay? You hate the rain … why did you come out tonight?"

His dad shakes his head, opening and closing his mouth a bunch of times as avoids his son's concerned look. Jérôme reaches out and puts a comforting hand on his shoulder. Édouard relents and looks up, eyes sunken and red with exhaustion. Determined, he opens his mouth, but Maxime interrupts before he can say anything.

"Jérôme, can I see you in the players' room? I need your help."

"Uhhh … sure thing," he answers uncertainty. "I'll see you soon, Dad."

He waves goodbye to his father before Maxime leads him into the maze of hallways that lead through the skating rink to the player's room. It's soon obvious that while the foyer of the building has been modernized and given a much needed facelift over the years, the hidden passageways of the arena have seen no such love. The tunnels smell stale and of decay, and the thick buildup of mold hides the paint which has chipped off in large flecks of eggshell. Dirt and grime line the ground, thick in the corners between where the walls and the cement floor meet. In a room off the main path, metal drags against stone and—for the first time since applying for the job—Jérôme's suddenly nervous inside the rink.

"I'm surprised the building looks this ... old," he admits out loud, his voice bouncing down the corridor and being swallowed by the silence at the end of the hall.

In the heart of the town, the building has always been a point of pride with the community. Built in 1943, it is the only historic site in the area left standing, and one of the few community buildings that is regularly maintained.

Or so he thought.

"It always looks like this at the end of the season. By the time another one starts, this place will look good as new. We just need to breathe some life into the place."

Soon, the players' room comes into view, and his shiver of anxiety is fast replaced with one of anticipation. The space is normally off-limits to anyone not on the team, and Jérôme can't help but walk so closely behind his boss that he nearly steps on his heels. His heart has never beat so fast, blood pumping in his excitement to finally see the spot where *Les Sangliers* prepare to do battle on the ice.

As he enters, a set of strong hands reach out and grab him, pinning his arms to his side.

"Hey! What the—"

Maxime picks up a thick bundle of rope, and begins wrapping it carefully around Jérôme.

"Very funny, guys. You got me. I don't really get the joke, but good job," he says, trying to laugh it off.

Maxime pulls the cord hard, letting it dig into the young man's skin, keeping his arms tight against his sides. When his boss doesn't laugh, he begins to panic.

Jérôme yells for help, trying to fight against the colossus and the bonds that keep him rooted in place. He lands a kick on the man's kneecap, and there's an audible *pop!* as something important dislodges from place.

"*Osti d' tabarnak de câlice de criss de marde!*"

The blow isn't enough to knock him down, and after Maxime is done roping Jérôme up, the two men carry him out of the players' room and onto the ice.

The townsfolk and community figures sit in the stands around the rink. When they see Jérôme being carried out, a hush falls over the crowd, before swelling into a cacophony of cheers and clapping. Some of them even stomp their feet on the ground, the echoes thundering through the arena. They leer at Jérôme from their seats, a ravenous animalistic energy pulsating around them.

They bring Jérôme closer to a giant hole, freshly bored into the centre of the rink.

The two men place Jérôme onto the ice and wave to the crowd. The boy writhes away from the hole, worming his body back to the locker room, but he stops when he sees the man stepping onto the rink.

Uncle Théo.

He glides towards Jérôme, footsteps silent on the cold surface, and the crowd goes wild, pumping their fists and whistling at the town's long-extinguished star. Théo, however, is far less enthusiastic. His gaze is far away and hollow, his shoulders hunched in submission. He wears his hockey pads and uniform, an old fashioned costume in modern times. His dead eyes look past Jérôme and into the ice, looking at something beyond what the others can see.

"It's that time of the year again, ladies and gentlemen," Maxime yells to the crowd, "where we offer up another sacrifice to the spirits that guard *Les Sangliers,* bringing us another year of success, prosperity, and rejuvenation for our community!"

The crowd claps and continues to stomp their feet in the stands.

"Thank you, Édouard, for granting us this opportunity. We know this can't be easy for you, but we hope you'll find comfort in knowing that, like Théo, Jérôme's spirit will live on and be with us. Always."

Jérôme screams, words spilling from his mouth and forming one desperate plea for freedom. He doesn't understand what's happening or, more aptly, he doesn't want to. He searches the seats for a face he trusts, for someone he knows will help, but even his father in the first row is a stranger to him. He's crying, not just tears of mourning, but tears of joy.

Jérôme looks away from him, but immediately wishes he hadn't. His eyes fall on a row of children standing near the audience. Like Théo, they look hollow and void of emotion. Their posture is slumped and concave, and their sunken eyes stare into the ice. A few of them shiver, cold without bodies to feel the chill in the air. Jérôme recognizes a few of them, but it takes him a second to figure out from where.

The arena.

They're all kids who worked the concession stand.

They're all kids like Jérôme.

"Théo, we hope this gives you the energy to have a great hockey year, and that our team can enjoy another lucky season," Maxime says. The audience howls with excitement as Édouard rises from his seat, descends the stadium steps, and cautiously steps onto the rink.

Jérôme begins to yell and thrash on the ice, trying to fight against the rope that keeps him immobile, but it's no use. The two men and his father slide Jérôme to the hole and lower him into the narrow opening in the rink.

He screams, but the sound he makes is swallowed up by the symphony of the crowd and the ice around him. The opening is narrow and tight, compressing his body and bruising his bones as the men push him below ground. A rib snaps as he's lodged into place, his screaming replaced by strangled gasps for air.

There's a low rumble and long groan, followed by a slow trickle of cold water from above. It soaks through his clothing, fills his ears and nose, and it's not long before it swallows him whole.

The last thing Jérôme hears through the water, as his lungs beg for air and the water freezes around him, encasing him in a tomb of ice, is his dad leading the chant for *Les Sangliers*.

Helena

It yells, the shrill scream growing louder as it echoes off the walls of the small room.

It must be hungry again.

If I had breath I would sigh, but I don't, so I just get up and walk into the kitchen. No, not walk. Shuffle. I can't fully move my feet like I used to, and it takes me a few minutes to sidestep the broken wooden chair in the doorway of the room. I approach the pantry and stop, trying to remember if the formula's there or in the fridge. It takes me a minute, spit from my open mouth rolling down onto my chin, before I'm almost positive it's in the cupboard.

I reach a shaky hand out, nails dragging against the wood until I finally find the small handle. I manage to wrap my fingers around it and pull the door open. There, on the middle shelf, sits the unopened pack of baby formula.

I found it at a bulk store—one of those stores people thought would make a great stronghold until the infection passed, but in reality was one of the first places in the city to become overrun—and then spent the next three hours trying to get it into the carriage, into the house, and into the pantry all while making sure little 'Na was safe.

Technically her name is Helena, but since I died a few weeks ago, speech has become increasingly difficult. I managed the whole name for a little while, then I called her 'Lena, and now it's down to the pitiful single-syllabled 'Na. And to be honest even that's exhausting to say. It's only a matter of time before I stop calling her something altogether and just start grunting at her.

I extend a hand, trying to pick up one of the cans, but end up pawing at the plastic-wrapped package. My shoulders sag; I forgot about the wrap. I slide the cans closer on the shelf and try cutting through the wrapping with my yellowing nails. It doesn't work, though, and I stare in disgust as two of the brittle nails crack and break off and fall pathetically onto the counter. I'm not actually repulsed, but I *am* concerned by the fact that it neither hurt nor bothered me.

I moan in frustration and, like a two-year-old in a grocery store that's been told they can't buy sweets, I flail my arms and throw my head back in a tantrum. Unfortunately, I haven't quite let go of the cans, something I only realize as they fly off the shelf towards me, hitting me in the face and then landing with a loud bang and a wet crunching sound on my foot. I look down: my big toe and part of my second one are completely crushed. Blood so dark it could be black is splattered on the floor and smeared on a few of the cans.

Wonderful.

On the plus side, the chipped toe polish that was bothering me is gone.

I feel my face to evaluate the damage: half of my bottom lip has been peeled back, bone and tooth exposed and bare.

The force of the fall is enough to split the plastic sheet on the cans, and a few of them go rolling across the vinyl tiles. I stumble after one, making sure not to trip on any of the others, and eventually pick it up with my dirty hands. I shuffle towards the stove, unhook one of the clean pots from the rack, and set it down hard on the glass stovetop. The surface has a deep scratch in it from the impact, but thankfully nothing is seriously broken. I pick up the can opener and spend what feels like a solid fifteen minutes trying to get it to hook onto the edge of the can.

If I wasn't already dead I'd have died of exhaustion.

Eventually, the blade cuts into the tin and I manage to open the formula and pour it into the pot without spilling *most* of it on myself. With the formula, the filth, and my natural scent of decay I must stink. Maybe that's why little 'Na 's crying so much. I thought she was hungry, but it's probably because I reek and she can't stand the smell. It's just another reason why I need to get Helena to safety.

It's just another reason why I need to get her away from *me*.

I turn the stove on and wait for the burner to heat up. This used to be the easiest part of taking care of Helena, but it's fast become the hardest. When I wasn't a sentient sack of meat I could tell when the liquid was warm enough for her to drink. Since I've lost the feeling in my limbs, since I've lost the feeling in *everything*, I can't tell when it's too hot.

I don't want to hurt her, so I've gotten into the bad habit of letting it come to a boil on the stove before letting it sit for twenty minutes. So far the system's been working, minus the ear-piercing shrieks 'Na makes while she waits for her food to be ready. It's a small price to pay, all things considered.

Once the formula comes to a boil, I turn the burner off and move the pot shakily to another spot on the stove for it to cool down. Then I make my way back to the living room in the hopes of entertaining 'Na long enough to keep her from screaming my head off.

As I move forward, I realize I'm now shuffling with a limp thanks to my butchered foot. As much as it's frustrating, I know it could be worse. I could be missing a leg, or half my body for that matter, and be forced to drag myself around on my hands. I just miss being, well, me.

The old me.

The *living* me.

I remember the days when I used to be able to see every shade of every colour, when I used to be able to feel the sticky sweat of my skin after a warm and humid day, when my sense of smell or my hearing weren't so sharp and painful. I used to love the time right between summer and fall, when the leaves were turning to maroon and amber but you could still smell lilac and freshly cut grass in the wind. Days when you could be outside in shorts without being too cold, but nights that were best spent in front of a campfire overlooking the Saint Lawrence River from your backyard, the light the sparks made against the night sky when they'd fly off the crackling logs and you could—

The grey walls of the small house amplify 'Na's already thunderous screams. I walk to the cradle and rock it slowly. I try to make soothing sounds, hoping to calm her until the food comes. It just sounds like I'm hissing and groaning at her. I'm about to stop when her shrieks turn into cries, and then those turn into passive gurgles of displeasure. We watch each other with curiosity, the cradle rocking gently and my body swaying in sync with it, 'Na hardly blinking and me not blinking at all.

She watches me with her big eyes, tiny hands reaching out to touch me, her curly hair poking out from beneath the edge of her cotton hat. She used to have the brightest eyes, but every morning they look a little duller, a little more empty. I don't know if it's because, like my memory, colours are slowly fading, or if it's because she is. I jerk my head side to side, trying to shake the idea out of my head.

Once I think enough time has passed, I let go of the cradle and move back into the kitchen, 'Na's cries slowly resuming. I pick up the pot of formula and carry it to the sink, then I take a plastic baby bottle out of the dish rack along with the teat—I cleaned them both meticulously the last time she fed—and slowly begin to pour the creamy liquid into the container. It's the hardest part of the whole process, and I move slowly in the hopes I'll be able to pour a little more accurately.

I don't.

Eventually, I exit the kitchen with half a bottle of formula and the knowledge that my daughter's going to be hungry again sooner than I'd hoped.

I put the bottle down on a nearby coffee table and pick a blanket up off the Lazyboy, which I then drape over myself. I don't want the grime, dirt, and blood that stains me to rub off on her. It's not that I'm worried about infecting her with, well, my *condition*—since the chemical runoff contaminated the water, we've all been infected, the poison only activating once the body dies—it's that I'm worried about getting her sick with something entirely *normal*. Now that I've begun the decomposition process, now that I'm harbouring all kinds of new bacteria inside of me, who knows what other diseases I might expose her to? I'm trying to shield her from my body as best I can, and I make sure to wash her with bottled water as often as possible, but I know it's not enough. With most of the hospitals shut down or inaccessible, there's no one to help 'Na if she gets sick. No one to make sure she's getting the right nutrients, no one to make sure she's healthy, no one to keep something as simple as a common cold from killing her.

It breaks my cold and still heart, but if 'Na stays with me, she's going to die before her first birthday and I won't be able to save her.

Once the sheet is in place, I awkwardly pull on a pair of gloves and pick up 'Na. I try not to move too fast, and I hold her as carefully as I can with what I hope is enough strength to make her feel safe without holding her tight enough to make her uncomfortable. I'm terrified to hurt her, I'm terrified to drop her, and I'm terrified I'm doing everything wrong.

I sit down with her in my arms and bounce her slowly on my knee, making sure she's well supported, and her crying dies down a bit. I pick the bottle up and place the teat near her mouth, which she gladly takes between her lips. She sucks at the formula in the bottle, making the smallest of gurgling noises. She shakes her little fists and kicks her feet while she drinks. Her cheeks glow, lips red from the bottle, and she looks so happy and out of place in the dark room. But soon, the formula is finished and her tears feel right at home in the gloomy space.

I turn to set the bottle down on the nearby table, but it's hard to move my body like I used to. My muscles are stiff and uncoordinated, and I jerk sharply to the left while lifting my right arm. My *wrong* arm.

The arm holding Helena.

I move fast, but not fast enough, as she slides out of my grasp and tumbles to the ground. Her forehead hits the wood flooring with a thud and her unhappy cries quickly turn into wails. I shout her name in surprise and concern—not her full name, never her full name any-more—and try to figure out how to pick her up. She's panicking and scared, and as my clumsy hands grab at her I know I'm only scaring her more. I'm worried about how badly she's hurt, but at least she's crying. I can deal with her cries; it's silence I would need to worry about. I manage to roll her over, her hands and feet kicking at me an-grily, and once she's on her back I move to scoop her up in my arms, but stop the second the smell hits me.

My stomach growls, saliva coating my mouth and slipping down the back of my throat as I stare at 'Na, my vision blurring at the edges.

Although there's just a small cut above her right eye and a split lip, because of my manhandling her face is streaked in the red liquid. It dribbles down her chin and rolls down her forehead and she screams, begging for someone—*anyone*—to pick her up and comfort her.

I stare at her for what feels like a long time as she cries herself hoarse and I force myself to pick her up, cradling the back of her head as carefully as I can as I lift her to my chest. I feel my stomach rumble and I close my eyes as I hold her against me, feeling the warmth of her little body against my cold one as she slowly starts to quiet down. I lower my face to hers, the scent of the blood almost too much, and pucker my lips to kiss her forehead. It's a difficult task to accomplish with part of my lip missing, and I end up pressing my lower teeth against her skin. I can practically taste the copper as I feel her tender flesh in my hands, and I don't realize I've opened my mouth or pressed her head against my teeth a little too much until she starts to cry again.

Horrified, I set her back down in her crib and collect her empty bottle before leaving the room as fast as my legs will carry me, tossing the sheet onto the couch as I go.

I drop the dirty bottle into the sink, rubber gloves still stuck on my hands from feeding 'Na, and stare at myself in the reflection of the kitchen window as the reality of my situation sets in.

My condition is getting worse.

I need to get my daughter to safety.

I can't stop myself from screaming at myself in the glass. I'm exhausted, even though my body can't get tired, and every second that Helena's with me marks my failure as her mom. She starts to cry again from the other room, no doubt caused by my outburst, and I try to focus on the next item in my to-do list: cleaning up Helena's blood.

I start to turn away from the windows to find what little medical supplies might still be in the house, but a figure outside the window stops me in my tracks.

A person.

No.

Something like me.

I try to figure out why anyone else would be here, tilting my head to the side like my dog used to do. The rest of the living have long abandoned this neighbourhood and all that's left is me and—

It hits me like a brick.

If I thought Helena smelled strongly to me, or that her screams were piercingly loud, I can only imagine how good she must have smelled to everyone in the area when I let her get hurt and how her wailing must have been like an alarm going off on a slot machine.

The man approaches the window and stares back at me, his face smushed against the glass as his milk-white eyes search the room for 'Na. I wait for him to go, to leave, to give up when he sees the room's empty of life, but he stays and he stares. As I watch him, something moves through the darkness, stumbling through the shrubs and over meticulously planted flowers. It's a woman this time, her face streaked with jet-black blood, and she marches up to the window and watches me too. There are more who follow behind the woman, and I realize 'Na's attracted a horde.

There's no time to plan, no time to think, so I don't. I just move.

I rush through the kitchen and back into the living room, prioritizing speed over coordination. I knock over a wooden chair and hit the doorframe hard enough that I break a rib, but I make it to my daughter with relative speed. My sudden appearance frightens her, but I don't have time to feel badly about it. I grab her from her crib and hold her face against my filthy shirt, hoping my stench will overpower her smell even though it won't.

As I clumsily navigate the living room furniture, I hear the kitchen window shatter from the pressure of the bodies gathered against it. A man rounds the corner. His nose is worn down to a stub and his right arm is hanging by a thread, and he launches himself at us. I turn and bolt, willing my legs into a sprint that puts me just beyond the man's reach. He crashes to the ground, his good arm reaching for my leg, but I manage to avoid it as I sprint to the back door.

As I approach the door, I panic and pray that the back locks are open and there's no chain to try and navigate. I hardly have the coordination to work the handle, I can't imagine having to navigate some kind of barricade too. Thankfully, my fears are unfounded, and I'm able to throw myself against the handle hard enough that it opens, and soon I'm running with Helena through the backyard.

I can hear them behind me, footsteps like rolling thunder, as I try to find my way out of the yard. At first, all I see is the fence, but then there's a gap of green where a set of hedges are and I throw myself at them, hoping brute force and numb flesh will be stronger than foliage.

As I push my way through the bushes, 'Na begins to scream even louder. Although she's shielded in my arms, the occasional branch snags on her clothes and scrapes what little skin she has exposed. I want to stop and tell her it'll be alright, I want to tell her I'll take care of her, but I can't stop. I can't talk. I just keep running as the scent of fresh blood attracts more creatures, like chum calling sharks to feed.

I finally burst through the green and sprint across the pavement, my bare feet slapping the road as I barrel through the rows of dead houses, trying to put as much distance as I can between 'Na and the unrelenting horde. My shoes fell off pretty early into my change and I'm thankful for it now; running would have been impossible with them still strapped on. As I move, I can't help but be grateful for my body that doesn't tire, that doesn't hurt, that doesn't feel. If I'd been alive, I'd never have been able to run so far so fast and still have the will to keep going. We'd have been eaten blocks ago.

As I round another corner, I hear them.

People.

Living people.

My heart jumps a beat and sinks all at once.

Helena will finally be safe.

Helena will no longer be mine.

These two truths exist simultaneously and are dependent on one another, and as much as I don't want to say goodbye to my girl before I've gotten to know her, I know it's the right thing to do.

Down the road, less than two blocks away, stands the group. They're huddled together looking in my direction as the noise of the horde follows behind me. But I have a substantial lead on the mass of flesh and bone that hunts 'Na down, and her future so close in front of me propels me forward. They stare at me, watching my every step, and as I get closer I move slower to not frighten them. I look down at

Helena one last time before I grip her tight and extend my hands, trying to say her name as I approach them.

"'Na!" I shout to them, holding the mass of tears and frustration away from my body. She's still crying, I don't think she ever really stopped, and I hope they can hear her pleas for help despite the roar of monsters approaching. "'Na!"

They watch me as I move, talking to each other in words that no longer sound familiar to my ears. One of them laughs, possibly at me.

"'Na!"

The horde is gaining on us and they still don't move to take her, so I walk faster, trying to find the balance between non-threatening and urgent.

"'Na!"

I can practically feel the bodies behind me, their vulture eyes on Helena in my outstretched arms. I'm running now as Helena shrieks, desperate for the people to get my daughter before the mob of sinew and meat does when it happens.

A loud bang.

Metal whistling through the air.

The wet impact.

Silence.

I stop running as my brain tries to make sense of the information that my heart already understands. My hands are wet and slicked with red, 'Na hangs still between them. There's a hole in my chest where the bullet entered, the metal still warm. I can't tell if it's hot from being fired or from taking the life of my daughter, but I don't care.

There's another loud bang and a body falls next to me. It's someone from the horde that's caught up with 'Na and me. Another bang. Another body. I should move, I should try to get out of the way, but I don't. I just slump to the ground and hold Helena against my chest, trying not to think about how damp her little clothes are.

The horde rushes past me, their sights set on the people waiting for them on the lawn, all interest in 'Na lost the second she stopped breathing. They walk past me, blind to anything but their hunger, and it no longer fazes me that I'll be like them eventually. If anything, I welcome it.

I sit there for what feels like a thousand years, the sea of bodies parting around me and moving to swallow the people whole when I feel her move.

I look down and watch as 'Na looks back up at me. She doesn't seem afraid anymore, just curious. She grabs a tiny fistful of my hair and flaps her hands excitedly, giggling as she accidentally rips off part of my skull and waves the hair around like a toy. I smile down at her, a big toothy smile, and for the first time in a long time, she doesn't cry when she looks back up at me. She just smiles and gurgles, laughing at nothing and everything, and for the first time since I died I laugh too.

I push myself to my feet, 'Na held firmly in my arms, and walk against the horde to take my daughter home.

CONQUEROR

Originally performed on The Wicked Library, *January 2018.*

"Go make me a sandwich, bitch!"

"Yeah, go make me a fucking sandwich," someone echoes, their voice loud in the headset and ringing in your ears.

"What a fucking noob," you snort, pausing momentarily mid-sentence to take a gulp of your neon-green fizzy drink before talking into the expensive mic once more. "Learn how to shoot or GTFO, comprendé?"

You're met with laughter mixed with the crackling of static from poor internet connections, and background noise from the other players.

"I'm trying to, but I can't—"

"—hit the wide side of your mother? Truuuuuuust, we know."

The kids howl with glee—the exception being one undignified "Hey!"—and you smile at your cleverness, leaning back in your leather chair as you watch the final kill-cam.

"Awwwww, there it is!" someone calls out, and you watch as your avatar—your gamer tag, C0nquer0r, glowing yellow over your souped-up futuristic soldier—jumps behind another player.

"Awwww shiiiiiit. You were playing as one of the new characters they added? No wonder I didn't recognize you," someone says over the channel.

"Fuck yeah I am. This one handles pretty sweet too. Might stick to using this melee one for a while."

You watch as your soldier knifes them in the back, ending the match.

"Yeeeeees!" a kid calls out, yelling over the sea of other voices. "That's what I'm talking about!"

"Way to fucking go, brah."

"*Obviously* you're the last kill of the round. Figures."

"Don't feel bad," you say, with mock sympathy. "Not everyone can be this good. Just feel honoured I've graced you with my digital presence."

"Ugh."

"So humble."

"Diiiiiiick."

"Whatever, dweebs," you say to the group.

"Dweebs? What are you, forty?" one of your friends—KMar94—jokes.

The group laughs at your expense and you swallow hard in annoyance.

"Shut up, you shit shooter. Don't you know retro's in? Get with the fucking times. C0nquer0r out," you say loudly, before powering the console down.

You take another swig of your drink, hating the overly sweet taste of it on your tongue, before pulling the headset off and getting out of the chair, the footrest springing back into place as you stand. You haphazardly brush crumbs from yourself with the back of your hand as you cross the room and put the controller and mic down on a shelf of the TV cabinet. You press the small button on the side of the massive screen, turning off the TV, and head to the kitchen to dump the remainder of the drink down the drain and chuck the can in the recycling.

The floorboards of the old apartment squeak under your weight as you lazily shuffle into the kitchen. You groan to yourself as you notice your phone on the coffee table's lit up with notifications and, with an even louder groan, you realize they're from your colleagues and you can't help but scroll through a few of them.

You were supposed to order more orange aprons for the store, reads one of the texts.

I need you to come in early tomorrow. Marion called in sick, so I need you to work the full day, reads another.

"Fuck off," you mutter to yourself, continuing into the other room.

You lean against the counter as you pour the green liquid into the sink, trying not to pay attention to the hissing noise the carbonation makes as it hits the metal, or wonder what kind of lasting damage it'll do to the inside of your stomach if you keep drinking it. You don't even like it; you'd only bothered to pick up a can at the convenience store near your house so you could finally know what it tastes like, and why the kids you talk to online like it so much. (It turns out the drink is a confusing mix of too much sugar and extremely sour candy).

You chuck the empty metal can into the small recycling bin beside your garbage can, and cross the cramped room to your fridge. You pull open the handle, which is still slick with a bit of grease from your supper the other night, and you take out the cardboard box of leftover chicken. You open the lid, your stomach rumbling, and groan in annoyance when you notice the food is past its prime, a few patches of white fuzz growing on the top.

"Waste not, want not," you mutter.

You grab a fork and a knife from a nearby drawer and slice at the chicken. When you're convinced you've excised most of the mold, you throw the good meat into a bowl, place it in the microwave, and heat it up as you chuck the box and the remainder of its contents in the trash. Before the two minutes are up, you take the bowl out and start shoveling food into your mouth unceremoniously. It's pretty bland, especially without any gravy, and it's definitely not hot enough, but you know it could be worse and so you're calling it a win.

As you chew your food, the kitchen silent but for the wet smacking of lips, you hear your phone start to vibrate from the other room. You ignore it, letting the call go to voicemail, but when it starts back up again you cave and decide to answer it. You put the bowl down and move quickly into the living room.

You check the caller ID and groan before answering

"Hello," you mumble into the receiver.

"Jesus fucking Christ I sent you like seven messages!" the man on the other end shouts. "You never put your phone down when you're at work, but you don't think to check it at home?"

"Sorry, I was in the middle of—"

"I don't care," he says, flatly. "I need you to come in early tomorrow and stay until closing."

"I have plans," you say, looking across the room at the console.

"Cancel them."

"But—"

"You're on thin ice. You're never on time, you don't do what you're supposed to, and God only knows why you think you can routinely call in sick. So don't push me. I need you to come in early. I need you to replace Marion. And unless you can prove to me that you have an appointment, a dead relative, or something that's genuinely important to go to, then I expect to see you there tomorrow. Otherwise, I'll be forced to find a new cashier who can be. Got it?"

"Yeah. Yeah, I got it."

"Good," your boss says, sounding tired. "I'll see you in the morning. *Don't* be late!"

He hangs up the phone and you listen as the line goes dead. You hold the phone to your ear longer than you need, knowing that by now the phone app has closed and your ear is pressing against the home screen. Eventually, you lower the device and put it back on the table. You hate your job, you hate your boss, and the idea of spending a day surrounded by annoying customers and colleagues who think they're better than you is enough to make your throat tight and your chest hurt.

You stare at the game system across from you and, not wanting to go to bed angry, decide you'll play and de-stress for a little while before calling it a night. You turn the television back on, press the start button on the remote, slip the headset in place, and flop down into your leather chair. You log into the game, picking your new favourite character from one of the menu screens, and join an online match already in progress, feeling a swell of relief as you're met with the sound of static and banter. Your gamer tag glows yellow in the top right corner of your screen, and you feel the tension melt as you slide back into your role as C0nquer0r.

When you play, you're a god to the kids you kill online. You can forget that you're a middle-aged cashier, you can forget the way your career went up in flames when you were spotted with a patient less than half your age, and you can forget the divorce your partner demanded when you were accused of sleeping with said patient. When you're plugged in, when you're C0nquer0r, you can forget how shitty real life is.

For a little while, at least.

"Hey, dumbasses. Miss me?"

You know something's not right even before you open your eyes. You can feel the uneasiness spread through you as you stare at the black of your eyelids, trying to pinpoint the source of your mounting anxiety. Opening your eyes, you move your head, trying to work the stiffness and kinks out of your neck. Your disorientation makes the room unfamiliar at first, and the second it clicks, you're filled with dread.

You're still in the living room.

You must have fallen asleep in your chair.

You look around and see that your remote has fallen off your lap and onto the floor, your headset resting beside it. The television and console are off, and it takes you a moment to piece things together. You were playing and got tired, and you wanted to keep going after a short break, but you must have nodded off instead.

You rub the sleep out of your eyes with one hand as you get to your feet, grabbing your phone from the coffee table. You press the home button and, when the screen stays black, you hold the power button down. An empty battery symbol flashes across the screen, and you grumble to yourself as you go into your bedroom to plug the phone into the charger by your nightstand. You wait another minute before holding the power button down, your phone slowly coming to life.

The screen lights up and you want to scream when you realize that it's 11:42 a.m., almost five hours later than when you were asked to come in to work. Then comes the flood of missed texts, voicemails, and even an email from earlier in the morning.

Thomas tells me you're still not in. Are you on the way?
06:57 a.m.

Where are you? Are you almost here?
07:03 a.m.

I told you not to be late.
07:48 a.m.

Answer your phone.
09:03 a.m.

Collect your things and drop off your apron by the end of the week.
10:28 a.m.

You open your inbox and realize that the message is a dismissal email from the company. They've sent you instructions on how to collect your possessions and leave your uniform, and a notice that your belongings will be thrown out if you don't come to collect them in a timely fashion. The message tells you that the date your insurance will end, your final pay, and your record of employment will be mailed shortly. They thank you for your hard work and wish you the best with your future endeavours, but kindly remind you that they do not provide references.

You're not sure whether to laugh or cry, whether to be outraged or grateful that you've finally been released from your boring, soulless job. On the one hand, you hated working there. The fact that everyone was so pleasant, and couldn't seem to differentiate between being colleagues and being friends, drove you mad. On the other hand, it was a job—something you desperately need—and the home improvement centre had been the only place that was willing to hire you after the rumours about your firing scandal had circulated the community.

You dial your voicemail, press play, and then delete the messages before listening to them. If the email and the million texts are any indication, the messages were probably left by one of the managers calling to give you shit and someone from human resources letting you know that they were firing you.

You want to whip the phone across the room, watch it hit a wall and smash into little pieces. You'd even settle for just crushing the screen, you're so angry. But instead you power down the device and return it to its spot on the nightstand. You take the pillow from your bed, hold it over your face, and scream into it. You know it's obnoxious of you—childish, even—but it helps relieve some of the anger threatening to push you over the edge.

You get up from your spot on the edge of the bed and head into the kitchen. You put a pot of coffee on and lean against the counter as it brews. You debate sleeping the day away, but decide against it. There are more productive ways to use your rage. As the coffee brews, you head into the washroom to clean yourself up. You take a quick shower, towel yourself dry, and throw on an old t-shirt and a pair of baggy sweatpants. You head back into the kitchen and pour yourself a large cup of coffee, taking a sip while it's still flaming hot and enjoying the way it leaves a trail of heat down your throat and into your stomach.

Now it's time to get down to business.

You turn on the television and the console, grab the remote, and crawl back into the leather recliner. The familiarity of the seat, the squeeze of the headset, and the weight of the controller in your hands put you at ease. The day's been rough, and you need a pick-me-up. The light on the machine glows green, and your pulse quickens as it signs you back into the game. You scroll through the characters, excited to see they've added someone new to the roster, and you select them as the game loads and finds you a group to play with. You smile as it drops you in the middle of a battle, and you feel instantly better as you fire a clip into an oncoming opponent.

"No waaaaaay!" someone calls through the headset.

"Oh shit, y'all! C0nquer0r's joined us!"

"Yup," you say with excitement. "You guys ready to watch a real pro play?"

"We're all dead," someone says into their mic.

"Aww sweeeeeet. You're playing as the new gunner they added!"

"You know it!" you say, struggling to make your voice sound right. It's hard sounding like a teenage boy on a normal day, and the effort of it strains your throat, but you'd rather sound like a teen than yourself so you force yourself. You've seen how vicious the online gaming community can be and you know what could happen if they decide to turn against you. Doxxing. Hacking. Permanent bans of beloved serves. You'd seen it all before.

You move your character forward, a thrill running through you as you start playing. You move your avatar across the map, dodging bullets and bombs as people are ripped to shreds beside you.

"You're never on during the day," KMar94 says through the mic, cussing under his breath as you shoot him.

"So?"

"So shouldn't you be at school or some shit?"

"Shouldn't you?"

He snorts. "Yeah, but I had my mom call me in sick before she left for work cause I 'wasn't feeling well.'" You can practically hear the air quotation marks.

"Savage."

"Why are you home?"

"Slept through my alarm."

"Idiot."

You can't disagree with him.

"Maybe ... but I'm an idiot that's gonna kick your ass."

"You're an idiot that's gonna *try*."

The two of you play a few more rounds of the free-for-all mode— each of which you most definitely win—before opting to play a few team rounds. Sure, there's not as much glory when you win with another player, but this kid just gets you. He understands you, even if he doesn't know everything about you, and it makes you happy. You swell with pride whenever you win a match, and you feel unstoppable. Hell, you *are* unstoppable. You're C0nquer0r, after all.

"These indie developers are mental, man," he says to you. "They keep adding new characters to the game, and updating glitches and shit. You don't see the big guys doing stuff like this. They make you spend a fuckton to get one—*one!*—shitty DLC character. And it's usually so glitchy!"

"Right?" you shout your agreement. "These guys are so good. Probably because they know we're, like, a super dedicated community or whatever. Like, there's not a lot of us, but we're all fucking addicted to this shit. Any word when they're putting out a sequel?"

"Naw. I don't think they're gonna bother, tbh," KMar94 says.

You barely dodge a bomb, his words leaving you upset. You can feel your freshly cultivated good mood already fading, the calm draining away.

"What? Why wouldn't they?"

"Well, 'cause like, I don't think people are playing it as much as you think they are. Like, I still love it, but I haven't seen XRayShooterz or KievMeABreak on for the last few weeks. And like, obviously the player pool is getting smaller. Why else would we have run into each other on here, you know? So like, maybe they're releasing new characters to try and get people back? I don't know."

"That's fucking bullshit," you say, angry. This game is everything to you. The thought of people abandoning it, abandoning C0nquer0r, makes you furious. "This is the best game of all time. End of discussion."

"For sure, brah. It's baller as fuck. Easily my favourite game."

A red counter shows up on screen, marking the approaching end of the game. You casually shoot at people, knowing you and your teammate are far enough ahead in this battle to take it easy.

"*Definitely* my favourite game. Like, none of the other first person shooters have such animated characters. Like, if they get shot, they look hurt. If they kill someone, you can actually feel the emotion in their face. This game is the tits man. I wish I could play it forever."

The timer reaches zero, the game coming to an end.

"Oh yeah?" KMar94 says through the mic.

"Fuck yeah. Definitely. Another game?"

"How about one on one?"

"Oh, what, tired of winning?"

"Ha ha," he drawls. "Okay, how about this: we play a versus, just the two of us, winner gets whatever he wants."

"Sounds like a plan. I love winning new shit."

You watch as he sets up the game. The timer starts counting back from ten, getting ready to signal a new round.

"If you win, you get to play forever. If *I* win, I get to play as C0nquer0r."

You roll your eyes—two seconds 'till go time—and smile.

"Sure, man. But fat chance of that happening."

A green "GO" flashes across your screen and your soldier takes off, sprinting to the nearest weapons cache and picking up your favourite shotgun and bowie knife, before moving through the map. You don't need to check the map, or deploy a heat-seeking drone to know where he's hiding. He's a predictable player—you've mentioned that to him more than once—and you're sure that, as usual, he's parked his ass behind one of the sand dunes on the edge of the map and is getting ready to snipe you. When you get close, you duck behind one of the dilapidated huts and throw a grenade at the dune, easily dodging the bullet you knew was coming. The grenade goes off, and you hear KMar94 curse on the mic, his character dead.

He respawns and you head to his new location, sure of his moves before he even makes them. Before he gets a chance to even pick up his rifle, you've shot him dead. The rest of the game plays out a lot like the first half, with him trying to run from your avatar, and you lying in wait for him at weapons caches or on rooftops. As the timer turns red and counts down the last few seconds of the match, you can't help but brag.

"That's what you get!" you shout through the mic. "That's the price you pay for messing with C0nquer0r. Suck it, bro!"

The game ends, and you can't take your eyes off the screen as it replays your final kill of the game. You smile to yourself as your soldier runs off a roof, sailing over the other competitor, and shoots his brains out from above. You can almost see the moment the other soldier knows he's going to be shot, what almost looks like a glimmer of annoyance passing over his face.

"Fuck yeeeeees!" you shout again. "Better luck next time, my man."

"No worries," he says calmly.

"So I'm thinking I want you to buy me this new skin I was eye-balling online, and maybe a new remote, cause the battery doesn't last on this one. Hope your mom doesn't mind you borrowing her credit card," you laugh.

"I'm not buying you anything," he says sternly. "I told you that if I won, I would get to play as you, but if you won, you'd get to play this game forever. It's pretty much win-win, so..."

"No, it's not. And I'm not giving you my logins, so stop being a sore loser. Now, should I fucking DM the webpages to you or shou—"

"I don't need your logins to play as you."

"I told you, I'm not letting you play as C0nquer0r. Fat fucking chance. Stop being a creep and pony u—"

"Stop talking," he says, voice deeper and distorted. You open your mouth to tell him something's wrong with his mic, but the words don't come. You try again, but still, you're silent. You try to reach for your throat, but you're frozen still. The TV flickers and you watch as KMar94's avatar fills the screen, smiling at you, and reaches a hand through the screen.

If you could, you'd be shouting, but you can't and so you stare as the soldier pulls his body through the frame of the flatscreen. As he materializes in your living room, his computer generated form is replaced with a solid human body, only the person standing in front of you looks nothing like the super soldier from the game. The tall mass of muscle is replaced with the short, wiry, build of a pre-teen boy. He looks delicate, almost frail, and what used to be a close-cropped military cut is now a mess of greasy brown waves. He straightens up as he approaches you and, although his movements seem relaxed, his eyes are filled with panic.

"You're so much … older than I was expecting," the boy—the thing?—admits to you. His voice is deep and whispery, and it definitely doesn't belong to the body it's coming from. "Or maybe you're *exactly* as old as I thought you'd be, and it's just KMar94 who's surprised by your age. I can't tell for sure."

You try to force yourself to your feet, try to fight whatever's keeping you fixed to your chair, but it's no use.

"That's not going to get you anywhere," he says. "A deal's a deal. You get to join all your friends and keep playing from now until forever. And now I also get to play as you. Like I said, everyone wins."

He reaches a hand towards you and the terror is so intense that you wonder if you'll throw up despite being unable to move. The boy grabs your throat and pulls you out of your seat, dragging you towards the television. You try to scream, try to fight, but you can only watch in horror as he reaches back into the television, the pre-teen body morphing back into a super soldier once more, and pulls you in with him.

"Awww shiiiiiiit! They added a new character," someone screams into their mic.

"Another one?"

"You only just noticed?"

"I'm not observant. It took me like a month to realize KMar94's tag was deactivated. Eat me. And fuck yeah! I mean, the armour's a little flashy, but yolo, right?"

The game timer flashes red, the match almost over.

"Ugh, yeah, that's like the brightest fucking blue they could have used for body armour. Like, ew, no. Control, alt, delete, please."

"I think it's pretty sweet," a fourth player says.

Your body is made to run, feet slipping on the sand as you try to get to the weapons cache in time. But you see the grenade heading towards you and know with certainty that you won't make it. It lands at your feet and explodes, ripping holes through your body and flaying skin from bone. You scream—no, you *try* to scream—as everything fades to black. The game ends for the players and the final kill cam is displayed. Your body regenerates, forced to go through the motions once more, forced to be torn apart once more, until the game is done and the players return to the menu. You fade to black and you could weep from the sudden reprieve, praying that you won't be made to play the next match.

"So, anyone want to play one on one?" a familiar voice asks the others.

"Yeah, sure. I'm a glutton for punishment, after all. So, which tag are you?"

You try to warn him, try to scream, but, as ever, you remain dead silent.

"C0nquer0r. I'm C0nquer0r."

FULL MOON RUN

Originally published in Sanitarium Magazine no. 34, *June 2015.*

It stirs inside me,

it compels me,

it calls me,

and echoes

echoes in my veins.

It's forcing its way out from

beneath the surface.

I can't

stop.

My skin rips, tears, breaks.

It's

s t r e t c h i n g

me

p u l   i n g me.

I breathe,

in,

out,

in,

out.

Waiting.

Finally my skin

spl its

  and I'm free.

My paws trample hard earth,

nostrils flaring,

my heart

beat beat beat beating

as I chase my

prey.

My teeth r i p into flesh,

bones breaking,

blood f

l

  o

w

   i

n

   g

My claws find muscle,

sinew,

hide,

and

  s

   c   t

   r l r

   a o e

   t n n

   c g c

   h   h

     e

     s through them.

I sleep,

exhausted,

in a bed of leaves,

blood still on my

tongue.

When I wake up,

it's in my prison.

A body,

e l b a z i n g o c e r n u

to me,

until the next full

m—n.

Highway 16

Originally published in Creepy Campfire Quarterly: Issue #3, *July 2016.*

He holds the wheel firmly in one hand and adjusts the brim of his Stetson with the other. The leather is old and worn, worked in by use and constant wear. Even though he bought the hat in Alberta, he swears the cowhide smells like Texas.

The radio plays one of his favourite country songs and he turns it up, drowning out the sound of the rain and bobbing his head in time with the music. He hums half-heartedly along with the tune, his gravel voice ripping the song to shreds in his mouth as he scans the road for signs of life.

His heater makes a long whining sound and stops pumping out hot air. The window begins to fog up, grey slowly creeping into his line of sight on the bug-smeared window. He grunts in frustration and slams his hand onto the dash. The heater gives an exhausted metal groan and turns back on, filling the pickup truck's cabin with heat once more.

He presses his foot down hard on the gas pedal and flies down Highway 16, drumming his hands on the wheel in time with the music.

The rain comes down in sheets, the windshield wipers having a hard time keeping up with the falling water. He navigates his truck around a bend, grimacing as the truck slides around the turn on the wet asphalt. He steadies his Ford and continues to drive towards Prince George.

Another song begins to play, but the signal's bad. The guitar and banjo twangs mix with the static and falling water to make an unpleasant melody. He reaches out a hand to shut off the radio and— with some alarm—watches as sunspots erupt across his skin. He stares as the skin on the back of his hand grows loose and wrinkled, his nails beginning to yellow.

The car begins to rattle and shake, and he turns his attention back to the road. He steers himself off the dirt shoulder and back onto the highway. He glances back at his hands—so much older now—and grabs the pair of lambskin gloves off the passenger seat. He pulls them on without looking, eyes focused on the road, the music still blaring.

Eventually, once he's found the courage, he glances at the time on the radio.

9:48 P.M.

His breath catches in his throat as he continues down the highway. He hadn't realized it was already so late, that it was already the final day of the cycle, or that he'd need to find another one so soon.

He keeps his course along the road, taking the turns slower as his vision begins to worsen. After a couple of kilometers he finally pops open the glove compartment and takes out his glasses. They're old and black rimmed, the lenses scratched and dirty. He braces the steering wheel with his knee and cleans them with the hem of his shirt. Once they're as spotless as they're going to get, he puts them on and takes the wheel once more.

He continues down Highway 16, passing an exit for a truck stop along the way. He doesn't see the sign—thick rain and bad vision keeping it hidden—and he drives right by it, his tank less than an eighth full.

His stomach growls and he immediately regrets skipping out on supper. He reaches around to the passenger's side, rifling through the piles of old clothing and random objects on the leather seat. He feels around until he finds a stale packet of Beer Nuts, and tries to rip it open with his teeth. His hands shake, and the effort of pulling the wrapper open sends sharp jolts of pain shooting into his gums. He drops the snack and grunts in frustration.

The light for the gas flicks to life and he beats his hand against the steering wheel, accidentally honking the horn. He continues down the road for another twenty kilometers before the pickup truck finally crawls to a halt by the side of the highway.

He lies his head on the wheel and closes his eyes, exhaustion flooding him and dread pumping through his veins. He sits silently in the cabin, the music filling the space around him. The noise in the cramped quarters make him claustrophobic, and when he can't take it anymore, he shuts the music off. He opens the visor and reluctantly checks himself in the small mirror.

His teeth are yellow and stained, his face lined with deep wrinkles, his golden hair now ash white. What used to be a strong, square jaw is now saggy skin and jowls.

But his eyes …

His eyes never change. Even when he's young his eyes stay old. He's seen and done too much in the hundreds of years he's been alive for his eyes not to show it.

He turns off the car, making sure only his hazard lights are on, and takes the key out of the ignition. He grabs his dark leather jacket and exits the Ford. He pulls on the coat—body cracking with age—and zips it closed before he gets completely drenched. He pulls his collar tight around his neck and adjusts his hat, a few stray droplets of water finding their way past the leather and rolling down his spine. It sends a chill through his bones, the arthritis he didn't have an hour ago beginning to flare up.

Locking the doors of the black pickup he begins walking down the highway, back the way he came. He walks slowly, shuffling along the side of the road. His shoulders are hunched over and his back is throbbing.

He keeps walking, body shaking and fingers numb. The rain beats him down, his steps getting slower and more painful. His pants are drenched, the water rolling down his pale legs and soaking the insides of his cowboy boots.

A bright light flashes in the distance and he closes his eyes tight, raising a hand to shield them from the brightness. He braces himself and waits for the impact, counting down the seconds until he hears the inevitable screech of brakes from a car stopping much too late.

But it never comes.

The vehicle gradually comes to a stop a few feet away from him and the driver shuts off the lights. He lowers his hand, blinking quickly to clear the spots from his vision, and his heart begins to pound fast as he hears a car door open and slam shut. Someone runs towards him and he smiles to himself as he hears an umbrella popping open.

"Sir? Sir?" a woman calls, over the rain. "Are you okay?"

The woman comes towards him and holds the umbrella over his head, shielding him from the rain. He nods his head and shivers, exaggerating the movements so she sees them in the dark.

"Sir, are you sure you're okay?"

After a moment he eventually shakes his head.

"My car ... It ran out of gas and I don't have a cell phone. I must have missed the sign for the gas station and now I'm all turned around," he says through chattering teeth. "I'm so sorry, but could you point me in the right direction?"

"Of course. It's down the road," she tells him, pointing in the direction of his pickup, "for another thirty kilometers and then you take the exit, continue for another three, and you can't miss it."

His face falls and he nods.

"Thank you dear," he says in the most melancholic voice he can muster. "I appreciate your help."

He smiles at her, turns around—wobbling a bit for effect—and starts heading down the highway the way he came.

It takes a few minutes longer than he'd expected, but the woman comes running up to him and shielding him with the umbrella once more.

"Sir, if you like, I can take you," she offers.

"No, no," he says quickly, "I can make it. I'll be fine."

"With all due respect, it's a long walk there and an even longer one back if you're going to be hauling fuel with you. It'll take you all night at the rate you're going. Please, let me help you."

He nods his head slowly with fake reluctance. She hands him the umbrella and runs back to her small car, starts it up, and pulls up beside the old man. She runs back out, takes the umbrella from the man, and holds it over him as he gets into the car, pulling one cramped leg in at a time. She throws the soaking wet umbrella onto the backseat before running around to her side—yet again—and getting in.

The pair drive down the dark highway and pass his truck, parked on the shoulder, lights flashing dimly.

"Is that yours?"

"Mhmm."

"It's such a big truck for such a small man! Don't your knees hurt getting in?" she asks.

"They do now, but they haven't always given me such a hard time. It feels like only yesterday that I was a much younger man," he chuckles.

"Time has a way of sneaking up on people."

He glances at the clock—*11:17 P.M.*—and nods.

"Yes, it does."

They drive the rest of the way in comfortable silence. She keeps her eyes glued to the road while he watches her from under the brim of his hat.

She's objectively beautiful: high cheekbones, copper skin, long black hair, and brown eyes that shine faintly in the light of the dashboard. He can't help but wonder how brightly they reflect the moon and stars on a clear summer night. She has full lips and a strong nose, but her chin is soft and round with only the hint of a cleft. He can't help but admire her beauty.

It's a kind he's fallen in love with over and over again for generations.

She turns her flasher on, even though no one's behind them on the road, and takes the exit off Highway 16. He stares as lights become visible through the rain in the distance.

"It's so different," he mutters to himself.

"Oh?"

"This area used to be nothing but forest," he tells her as she pulls up to one of the gas pumps, shutting off the car. "There was nothing but trees and wild animals."

She laughs politely and shakes her head.

"You must be thinking of somewhere else. This area's been developed since before I was born. My grandparents used to complain about how the nearby town was always expanding."

"Trees and wildlife," he says with a raised voice, "that's all that used to be here. When I came over from England they'd just begun to settle this area. It was an interesting time to be alive. Everything felt ... new."

The woman shifts in her seat, and her voice sounds too high when she speaks.

"Sir, I think you're getting yourself mixed up. Too many history books, and age can be cruel. My grandmother used to have problems with that."

"I'm not mixed up, you stupid bitch. I traveled to Fort St. James from London. They promised us all a better life and a world of possibilities," he says, staring at his reflection in the window of the car door.

He looks like he's in his eighties now, his hair thin and missing along his crown, sunspots marking his face. Deep bags hang under his cold green eyes and his lips are thin and reptilian. He looks away, disgusted.

"I didn't want to come here," he explains. His voice is rough and steady, all traces of confusion and fear gone. "I wanted to stay in London, but people—my family—were starting to notice how ... unchanging I was. I needed to start all over again."

The woman leans away from him—eyes darting between the man beside her and the light coming from the inside of the service station— and places one hand on her belt buckle and the other on the handle of her door.

"Sorry," he says, "I think you're right; I'm not feeling myself. Between the rain and the long walk, I've had a terrible night. I'm so sorry, dear." He covers his face with a hand and shakes his head. "I sound absolutely crazy, don't I? Oh Lord, I've turned into my grandfather. I'm so sorry if I've made you uncomfortable."

"Don't worry about it. You've been through a lot tonight," she says fast, pulling the door handle and turning her attention to the light across the gas station platform.

As she looks away, he takes off one of his lambskin gloves and, as she turns back, he places his bare hand to the side of her face. The touch sends a chill running through her skin, rippling through her body from the point of contact. She tries to move, but finds herself unable. She tries to scream, but her mouth only hangs open in a silent "O".

"I really am sorry," he says, voice anything but sincere, "but I didn't know the other girl was sick. I didn't know she had so little time to borrow."

He smiles as the sunspots and wrinkles fade from his skin. His hair grows back thick—white strands turning into golden waves—and his hanging jowls tighten into a strong jawline. Arthritic and stiff joints find release, his hunched back straightening out, and his eyesight comes back sharper than before. She watches, transfixed, even as her sight begins to dull, as the eighty year-old changes to a young man.

Her breathing slows, each inhale a strain on her body. She can feel her blood pumping through her veins at a snail's pace, as panic floods her senses. She feels like she's drowning in slow motion as her body shuts down one part at a time, twitching and writhing until it's still and all that's left alive is her mind—thoughts swirling in terror and fury at her own death. Soon, the synapses in her brain stop firing, and she's still.

The man removes his palm from her face and licks her sweat from his hand. He opens and closes his hand, admiring the way taut muscles moves under the healthy skin, and tries to shake the pins and needles from his arm. It's the same unpleasant sensation every time he drains someone. Still, remembering his aged reflection in the window of the car, he knows it could be worse.

It almost was.

He fixes his clothing, arranging it to hang properly on his sturdy form, and pulls his glove back on. He gets out of the car and reaches through to the driver's seat, pulling the woman's lifeless body onto the empty chair. It takes some effort to move her body and she sits awkwardly in the seat, limbs bent at uncomfortable angles. He arranges her to look as normal as possible, and closes the door.

He crosses the empty lot to the service centre. The employee behind the counter is staring down at his phone, laughing at something on the screen, and doesn't bother to look up as the man roams the aisles. He grabs a bag of chips and a plastic gas canister, then brings them to the register.

The gas station attendant pauses his video and looks up, stifling a yawn.

"Find everything?"

"Mhmm," the man says, pulling out a few bills from his wallet and pointing to the car in the lot. "Can you add fifty bucks for gas?"

The employee nods and rings up the total. He takes the money from the man's gloved hand and gives him back his change.

"Safe driving, eh? It's pretty bad out there."

The man smiles, pocketing the remainder of his cash.

"I think the worst is behind us."

He grabs his stuff off the counter, tips his hat to the kid in thanks, and walks back out to the car.

He opens the passenger door, tosses his snack on top of the dead woman, and slams the door shut before turning his attention to the gas pump. He takes the nozzle and puts it into the bright orange container, filling it to the brim. He puts the nozzle back on the pump, places the container on the floor of the passenger's seat, and climbs into the driver's side. He adjusts the seat, the mirrors, and arranges the steering wheel so it's not pressing into his knees before making his way back onto Highway 16.

About halfway to his truck the man pulls the car over, gets out and walks to the woman's side. He throws his food onto the dashboard and grabs the body by the hair, pulling her out of the car. Her body falls onto the shoulder of the road and she watches with wide, empty eyes as he grabs the back of her jacket and drags her through the mud. Once he's at the edge of the ditch that borders the gravel strip, he kicks her in. The Indigenous woman watches as he drives away in her car, staring after him long after he's gone.

Once he gets to his black truck, he dumps the gas into the tank and hops into the cab of the Ford. He leaves the woman's car unlocked and running, not bothering to shut it off before continuing on to Prince George.

As the rain finally begins to stop, he can't help but wonder if they'll find her come morning. If someone will see her body—cold and alone—begging to be found like the other nineteen were, or if the British Columbian wildlife will devour her body like they have countless others.

He looks at the glowing green clock—smiling for the first time in days at how much time he now has—and blasts the radio as he flies down Highway 16, heading home.

MR. PERFECT

Originally performed on The Wicked Library, *October 2015.*

She walks to the counter by the window, her wool slippers creating a static charge on the carpet, and takes a mug out of the cupboard. She picks up the nearby sugar jar and measures out two even teaspoons into the cup. Miranda grabs the coffee pot from the machine, the glass scraping against the burner and the liquid sloshing inside, and pours it into the mug. She stirs it all together and takes a sip, the hot coffee burning her tongue.

She stares out the window, enjoying the view of her street this time of year. The trees have gone from their deep shades of green to a romantic mix of red, yellow, and orange. The wind rattles the branches, shaking loose the dead leaves and sweeping them down the street. Halloween is only a few days away, and Miranda admires the decorations of the nearby homes. While it's never been her favourite holiday, Miranda can't help but feel sad she'll be missing it this year. She always enjoyed seeing the kids in their costumes, their plastic pumpkin buckets heavy with candy.

She shakes her head, snapping herself out of her daydream. She's sad to be missing it this time around, but she knows it'll be even better next year. They'll have settled into their new home by then, with (*hopefully*) a baby on the way, and their furniture company well off the ground.

Or at least that's the plan.

She watches her neighbour set up his scarecrow in his front yard, and groans.

"You owe me five bucks," she says loudly.

"What?"

"You owe me five bucks."

Patrick walks out of the bedroom in his boxers, the elastic over-stretched and torn at the hem, and stands behind her at the window.

"Fuck," he mutters, watching as Mr. Perfect, that's what they'd come to call him, arranges his plastic gordes around the scarecrow.

"He's single-handedly going to keep this house from selling," Miranda tells him.

"He's not going to keep it from selling."

"Would you really want to buy a house knowing *that* was going to be in the yard next to yours?"

Patrick decides it's a question better left unanswered.

The thing's hideous and unlike any scarecrow he's seen before. Its brown, leathery skin looks sunken in and dried out, and it wears a dress made of burlap. Its hair is yellow and straw like, framing its hollow face and black eyes, and its mouth is sewn shut with old twine. Even though Patrick knows it can't say a word, it looks like it's begging for someone to help it off its wooden post.

"It's not like he has crops to protect. The only thing he's going to scare away at this rate are buyers."

Patrick laughs and kisses the back of her head before going back to the bedroom and lying down on the uncomfortable inflatable mattress. They had shipped their bed with the rest of their furniture to their new home in Dundurn, Saskatchewan. Neither of them had wanted to sleep on an air mattress for a week while they waited for their belongs to arrive, but the thought of a thirty-two hour drive from Montreal to Dundurn with a bed strapped to their car had been even less appealing.

"You can't go back to bed," she says, walking into the bedroom after him. "You have to go over there and talk to him."

"Miranda, it's a tradition. He's put that thing up every year since we bought the house."

"I'm not asking him to take it down forever, I just want him to take it down until we find a buyer. Please, can you go talk to him?"

When he doesn't answer, she puts her empty cup down on the ground and climbs into bed, draping an arm across his chest and rubbing her cold feet against his warm ones. They lie together in comfortable silence until their backs begin to hurt from the squishy bed, then eventually get up to get dressed.

"I need to pass by Max's place to get the last of my power tools," he finally says, as he pulls on a pair of jeans and flannel shirt, "then I have a few errands to run. While I'm out go over and ask if he'll take it down. If he gives you a hard time I'll talk to him when I get back, okay? I'll even grab dumplings from that Chinese place you like."

She rolls her eyes as she gets dressed. She isn't happy about his proposal, but she doesn't reject it either. After a minute of silence she finally nods her head.

"God, I hate talking to him," she mutters, heading for the entrance-way.

"Why? Doesn't it interest you when he talks about weeding and lawn care? I sure know *I'm* riveted."

She laughs, voice bouncing off the empty walls.

"Try not to be too long," she shouts, as she pulls the door closed behind her.

Patrick pulls the Chevy into the driveway and puts it in park. He looks at the lawn next door and frowns, staring at the scarecrow in the fading sunlight, before finally turning the engine off. He grabs the stack of folded boxes and the bag of Chinese food off the seat next to his and gets out of the car, shutting the door hard behind him and locking it with the remote as he heads up the front path. Patrick slides his key into the front door and turns it, surprised it's already unlocked.

A burnt and bitter scent assaults him the second he's inside, and he buries his nose in the collar of his shirt as he closes the door behind him.

"Fuck, what's that smell?"

He walks through the hall to the kitchen and sees the pot of coffee bubbling on its burner. The water has long evaporated, a dark brown sludge left to burn at the bottom of the glass. He tosses the bag of Chinese food on the counter and drops the packing supplies on the floor. He turns the machine off and removes the pot from the burner, placing it in the sink.

"Miranda?" he calls, walking through the empty bungalow.

She's nowhere to be found.

He fishes his cell phone out of his pocket and dials her number, waiting for her to pick up. He hears a noise from the bedroom and curses as he recognizes her ringtone. He looks around the room, eyes resting on the hideous scarecrow outside his front window.

Patrick walks outside, shutting the door hard after him, and crosses the lawn to his neighbour's porch, not bothering with the walkway. He hopes Mr. Perfect doesn't notice the trampled grass and rings the doorbell. He waits a few minutes and rings the bell again, holding it longer this time. No one answers. He knocks on the door, his hand beating against the wood until his knuckles are sore, but nothing. He grabs the handle and gives it a push, but the door's locked.

He turns to walk back down the path, debating where to look next, when he notices the gate to Mr. Perfect's backyard is ajar. Deciding it's worth a look—maybe he's outside and can't hear the bell—Patrick walks past the fence and around the side of the house to the back patio.

But no one's there.

He turns to leave, eyes searching the perfectly green yard one last time, and stops in his tracks when he spots Miranda. Only she's not in the backyard, but in the kitchen, naked, tied up … covered in salt, her lips sewn together with twine.

"Miranda!" he screams, picking up a decorative lawn gnome and whipping it through one of Mr. Perfect's sliding back doors. The glass crashes to the floor, some of the smaller shards landing in the salt around Miranda and cutting her bare body.

Patrick rushes towards her, crouching on the ground and pushing piles of salt from her dehydrated skin. He grabs at the rope around her wrists, trying to loosen the knots and free her hands. Miranda makes a noise, something caught between a scream and a whimper, and before Patrick can feel the object collide with the back of his head, his world fades to black.

"You had every opportunity to go home. You had every chance to turn around. But no. You had to snoop. You had to stay."

Patrick blinks his eyes open against the harsh fluorescent light of the kitchen. He stares up at the ceiling, his senses returning to him one at a time.

"I was doing you a favour, is what I was doing, and you go and ruin it."

Mr. Perfect's voice sounds muffled and far away, like he's talking through an empty metal can.

"I was married to someone like her. 'Donald, mow the lawn,' 'Donald paint the garage,' 'Donald, we need to weed the yard,' 'Donald the bathroom's a mess,' 'Donald, the decorations,' 'Donald, Donald, Donald!'" he shouts, spit flying and hitting Patrick in the face.

He tries to wipe it away, but his hands are tied behind his back. He struggles against the rope, but it only chafes his wrists. Mr. Perfect comes into view, glaring down at him with wild eyes, a fishing hook threaded with twine in one hand. Patrick blinks, the light hurting his eye and his head pounding.

"She comes over here, she thinks she can tell me what to do. Thinks she owns me. Thinks she owns me like my wife did!" He shakes his head violently. "I do own you," he yells to himself in a high pitched voice, "you worthless, stupid old man!"

He grabs Patrick's face, holding it still with one arm, and pushes the fishing hook through his lips. He pulls the twine through Patrick's skin, strands of rough cord dragging through the fresh wound. Patrick screams in pain, lips pulling open along the twine, but his neighbour grabs his mouth harder and pulls the string taut, forcing his mouth shut.

"Don't you talk to me like that, you stupid bitch! You can't tell me what to do anymore. You got that, Lizzie?" he screams.

Miranda watches as Patrick's mouth is sewn to resemble her own, and the two of them writhe against their bindings.

Once Mr. Perfect's done with Patrick, he stands up and drags two heavy bags of road salt towards him. He cuts them open, dumping the contents on top of Patrick's naked body and disappearing from view once more. Patrick squirms, trying to get the salt off his body, but Mr. Perfect returns with two more bags that he adds to the heap, then another two, and still another.

"That was supposed to be for her," he points to Miranda, "and the driveway. 'Donald, remember we need extra salt for the pathway this year. Your parents always have such a hard time,'" he mimics again. "Dammit, Lizzie, I'll buy more!" he shouts.

He leaves the room, arguing amongst himself, leaving Miranda and Patrick to watch in horror from their salt mounds.

"I still can't believe how cheap we got this place," Hailey says as she unpacks one of the large moving boxes.

"Well it's been on the market for over a year. I think the bank was just happy to get rid of it," John admits.

She stares out the window, smiling at the golden leaves on the trees and the Halloween decorations.

"Those are hideous," she says, smile fading as she points to the yard next door. A chill runs down her spine.

Three scarecrows stand in the middle of the lawn; their mouths sewn shut, eyes replaced with black buttons, their arms delicately bent around a slate of wood and nailed into the post that holds them upright.

Her husband looks out and shrugs.

"They're not great, but it could be worse."

Hailey stays quiet as she stares out the window. John crosses the room and stands behind her, wrapping his arms around her and placing his chin on her shoulder.

"If you don't like them, you can always ask him to take them down."

"Yeah," she nods slowly. "Yeah, I think I will."

WHITEOUT

Originally published in ABANDON: 13 Tales Of Impulse, Betrayal, Surrender & Withdrawal, *October 2015*.

Joanne holds her hands firmly over Maria's eyes and guides her through the doors of the barn, making sure she doesn't trip on the wooden step or one of the cracks in the cement floor. She guides her past small mounds of hay, which have been covered in snow that's leaked through the gaps in the roof, and stops.

"Ta-da!" she sings, removing her hands from Maria's face.

Maria stares at the large stall in front of her; the walls are grey and worn—the paint coming off in flakes—and there's a hole in the wall closest to her. The door is broken and falling off its hinges and the floor in front of it is badly warped.

"Don't worry, we'll get that fixed," Joanne offers, pointing to the gaping hole. "Apparently the last owner's horse got spooked during a grooming and pulled the ring its halter was secured to right out of the wall."

Maria nods slowly.

"But we'll fix it."

"The walls or the rings?" Maria asks.

"Both. I mean, we'll need to overhaul the stables—just look at them—but it's going to be so great when it's finished."

Joanne watches with a bright smile as Maria walks around the barn. She pulls her scarf tighter around her, trying to keep the cold air from clawing its way into her parka. She rubs her hands together, her wedding band cold as ice and sticking to her skin, and silently wishes she'd been smart enough to bring her gloves and hat.

"It's going to need a lot of work," she tells Joanne as she makes her way back to the first stall.

"Yeah, but once the snow melts I can start working on everything. That way, I'll be able to spend the next few months planning all the renovations and passing out pamphlets in Westport."

"It's going to be expensive."

"That's what our savings are for."

"Our savings are supposed to get us through the winter now that you're not working," Maria counters.

"I am working, I'm just not making any money. Yet. Once this riding program takes off you won't have to write for that shitty magazine anymore and you can start working on your book."

Maria closes her eyes and smiles, imagining the picturesque life she's always wanted: mornings spent writing on the porch, apple pies cooling on window ledges, and the fresh country air. She lets out a small sigh as Joanne wraps her arms around her waist and rests her chin on Maria's shoulder.

"It'll be wonderful. I promise," Joanne whispers, before softly kissing her cheek.

"It better be," Maria teases. She moves out of Joanne's grip and heads over to the heap of firewood in the corner of the barn. She starts piling logs on top of each other in a neat little stack.

"What are you doing?"

"Rowing a boat," she jokes. "Obviously getting firewood. It's going to storm tonight."

Joanne shakes her head.

"Don't bother. It's not supposed to be bad, plus we have a few logs left in the mudroom if the heater's not enough for us."

"It's not going to be enough."

"It'll be plenty," Joanne tells her. She walks over to Maria and kisses the top of her head before leaving the stable and heading back to the house.

Maria gets up, dusting off the knees of her jeans, and heads to the door of the barn to admire the land. Nothing but snow-covered fields as far as the eye can see on one side, and the edge of a forest on the other. A few stray trees litter the property, and she watches, transfixed, as trees bend and branches snap in the unrelenting wind. She looks up at the sky, black clouds rolling in fast from the north, and it sends a shiver through her bones.

Once the cold becomes too much, she follows Joanne back down the icy path and into their home.

It takes her a while to get her winter boots off, working the knots out of the laces while working the cold out of her fingers. Her cheeks are bright red and her long black hair is tangled from the harsh winds. She pulls her boots off, nearly taking her thick wool socks off with them, and places the Merrells on a rubber mat by the door.

The mudroom is cold and smells like lumber. Coat hooks line the walls from which jackets and snow pants hang. There's a small bench facing the large window by the door, and boxes full of outerwear litter the floor. Maria stands, hangs her coat on one of the hooks, and opens the door to the house.

Warmth rushes her, and she smiles as the heat works its way into her skin while she closes the door of the mudroom behind her.

"What are you making?" she asks Joanne, who's busy working behind the kitchen counter.

"Hot chocolate, from scratch. None of that powder shit."

"I knew there was a reason I loved you."

"And all this time I thought it was because of my long legs and big brain. My life's been a lie."

Maria laughs as she walks through the kitchen to the large oak table in the dining room. She pulls out one of the heavy chairs and takes a seat, sidestepping unpacked moving boxes in the process. She opens her laptop and presses the power button, waiting for it to boot up.

"Did we put the mugs away yet?" Joanne asks.

"Uh, I don't know. I don't think so."

She drums her fingers on the table, waiting for the login screen to load. Eventually it chimes to life, asks her for her password, and starts up. She double clicks the internet icon and frowns when it gives her an error message. She refreshes the page with the same outcome. She closes her web browser, turns off her WiFi and waits a few minutes before trying to connect again.

Unable to Connect to the Internet.

She takes out her cell phone and opens her browser, hoping the homepage loads.

Unable to Connect to the Internet.

"Damn it," she mumbles to herself.

"What's wrong?"

"WiFi's down. I can't get it to work on either of these," she says, pointing to her old computer and even older phone.

Joanne sets the two bowls she's carrying down on the table and takes out her smartphone from her back pocket.

"I'm gonna take it you can't find the mugs," Maria chuckles, pointing to the large glass bowls full of hot cocoa.

"Yup. And I can't connect either. Did you need to do anything important?"

"No," she sighs, shutting the lid of her computer, "not really. Maybe I should unplug the router for a bit and try again a little later."

"I don't think that's the problem," Joanne tells her, nodding towards the kitchen window.

The sky, which was dark only a little while ago, is black as night. Thick storm clouds block out the sun and sheets of snow begin to fall on the farmlands. The wind—angry now—whips the snow up and throws it hard against the small house.

Maria tries using her phone—first attempting to use her data to check her email, then trying to call out—with no success.

"I thought you said it wasn't going to be bad," Maria says.

"It wasn't supposed to be."

The two of them sit at the table sipping their hot chocolates in silence as the wind howls outside, the windows shaking. The lights flicker and Maria begins to fidget anxiously with her ring. Eventually she gets up, goes to the thermostat, and turns up the heat.

"You're cold?" Joanne asks.

"Yeah, do you mind?"

"No. Go ahead."

She turns the dial, waiting for a click that'll let her know it's working, but the thermostat stays silent.

"How high are you putting it on?" Joanne calls from the table.

"It's not working."

Joanne gets up, the chair scraping against the floor.

"What do you mean it's not working? It's been on all morning and it's on now."

"It won't go any higher. The thing isn't clicking."

Joanne moves towards the dial and begins turning it, Maria stepping out of her way. When the heater still doesn't work, she turns it off—the thermostat clicking as it shuts down—and turns it back on slowly.

Nothing happens.

Maria crosses her arms over her chest, grinding her teeth together as Joanne continues to fiddle with the dial.

"Did you just turn the heat off?"

"Yeah, 'cause I'm trying to get it to work."

"It was working before."

"You said it wasn't!"

"I said it wasn't getting any hotter, you said it was working fine, and now it's not working at all!"

"We'll get it fixed."

Maria grunts in response and walks out of the kitchen, into the small living room. She picks up a blanket off the recliner and drapes it around herself. She sits down legs crossed, and remains silent as Joanne continues to play with the thermostat, cursing when it doesn't work.

Maria begins to pick at one of the small tears in the upholstery of the chair. She wheedles a finger into it, playing with the worn fabric and picking at the loose strings.

"You're going to make it worse," Joanne says, leaning against the doorway.

"Don't worry, we'll fix it," she tells Joanne, over enunciating her words and staring at the armchair.

"I don't know why you're getting worked up over the heater. We can just light a fire."

Maria doesn't answer her; instead she continues to pick at the fabric in silence.

"I know this isn't your dream house."

"No shit."

"I know you're thinking—"

"I doubt you know what I'm thinking right now, Joanne."

"I know you're thinking," she presses on, "that the reason we got this property so cheap is because everything's falling apart or broken to shit, and now you're wondering if it was worth it."

Maria stops picking at the fabric but doesn't look up.

"And I know you miss the city, and your family, and your friends."

Maria finally looks up.

"You're not the only one who misses everybody, and you're not the only one who wonders if moving out here was a mistake. I mean let's face it; we know *nothing* about living on a farm. I get horses, sure, but I've spent all of my life in a condo. I'm just as lost and scared as you are."

Joanne crosses the room and kneels in front of Maria, putting her hands in her lap. She catches Maria's eye and smiles.

"But I know it's all going to be okay. 'Cause I have you."

Maria laughs and slaps the top of Joanne's hand lightly.

"Oh, go start a fire you sentimental—emphasis on the mental—suck-up."

Joanne gets up, giggling, and heads out of the den to bring back firewood.

"You're so stupid," Maria calls after her. "And if you can't fix the thermostat, then call someone who can!"

She hears Joanne sigh from the hallway and listens with satisfaction as she changes direction and heads upstairs to the telephone in the bedroom instead.

Maria gets up off the recliner and walks back to the kitchen, still draped in her thick blanket. The walls look like they haven't been touched since the '70s, and she can't wait to remove the ugly wood paneling and slap a coat of fresh paint on them. She picks up her bowl of hot chocolate on the way into the room and gulps the last of it down, enjoying the feeling as it heats up her belly. She walks over to the sink and fills it with warm water and dish soap, watching as the bubbles fill the stainless steel tub. She drops her bowl into the water, a few droplets splashing onto her face and plaid blanket, and she stares out the window.

There's nothing but white as far as the eye can see. The once-black sky is hidden from vision as thick snow falls heavily and is blown hard against the glass, which rattles and shakes in its frame. Heat rises off the hot water and steams up the window. Maria runs her palm over the glass, wiping it away, but leaving small streaks in its place. She looks back out.

There's someone there, standing alone in the darkness, looking in.

Maria stares out at the figure, trying to make sense of it. At first she thinks it's just the snow and her wild imagination, but the longer she stares the more certain she is that there's really someone there. It stands unmoving, arms by its side, head tilted sideways, and she feels unnerved as she imagines it watching her back.

"Phones are down," Joanne says, feet silent on the stairs.

Maria jumps at the noise and clutches her chest.

"You okay?" Joanne asks.

Maria chuckles and nods her head, looking at her from over her shoulder. "Fine. You scared me is all."

The two of them chuckle and Joanne walks through to the mud-room. Maria looks back out the window, but the figure is gone.

The door of the mudroom slowly opens, creaking from age and disuse, and Joanne returns. She kicks the door closed behind her with a foot, her arms practically overflowing with firewood. Maria turns her attention to Joanne, who heads to the den, her woolen socks trailing dirt and flakes of wood. Eventually Maria turns back to the window and, to her surprise, the figure has returned.

Only now it's closer.

"Joanne," she calls, "there's someone out there."

"Doubt it," she shouts back from the other room.

The figure takes a step forward, its legs dragging through the snow as it approaches the house. It moves carefully and agonizingly slow; each step deliberate and unrushed. It tilts its head upwards, and Maria feels its eyes on her.

"No, there's someone out there!"

There's a loud thump as Joanne drops the firewood by the hearth, then the soft padding of her feet as she moves into the kitchen. She stops by one of the dining room windows and looks out into the field.

"I don't see anything."

Maria turns towards her, taking her eyes off the ever advancing figure, and motions for Joanne to come to her.

"You won't from that angle, but come here," she says.

Joanne skips around the table as Maria turns back to the window.

"See?" Maria asks, pointing to the man in the shadows.

"No. I can't see anything but white."

"He's right there!" she cries, turning to Joanne. "Can't you see him?"

"Sweetie, I'm really not seeing this thing you're seeing."

Maria looks back out the window, but the figure's gone.

"That's because it's not there."

"So you were imagining things," Joanne laughs.

"No," Maria objects, her voice stern, "I wasn't. There was someone there, but they're gone now."

Joanne's sceptical and nods her head slowly, rubbing the small of Maria's back. She looks back out the window, squinting to see if she can make out the figure, but all she can see is snow.

"Maybe you're right," Maria says, cutting through the silence. "It was probably nothing … Can you go start a fire? I'm cold."

"Sure. Wanna come help? It'll help take your mind off things."

"Sure, I'll be there in a second."

Joanne smiles, leaving the kitchen. Maria watches her go, pulling the blanket even tighter around her small frame and—with her heart in her throat—turns back to look out the window.

Nothing but white.

Maria tries to breathe a sigh of relief, to convince herself the figure was all in her imagination, but she can't. Because even though she doesn't see it, she can still feels its eyes on her.

The wind is like wolves at their door, howling and scratching to come in. It whistles in triumph as it forces its way in through cracks in their roof and the spaces in their window frames. The snow beats at their house, throwing itself at the walls and pounding on their door. The two women watch the chaos outside through their patio doors as they sit on the floor in front of the softly glowing fireplace.

"This is really bad," Maria says, desperately wishing the lights would turn back on.

"It's going to be fine."

Maria glares at Joanne.

"No, it's not."

"Storms happen."

"We never had one this bad in Toronto," she counters. "It was cold, and it was icy, but it was never this bad. And if it was—which it wasn't—we weren't in the middle of fucking nowhere without power or cell service."

The fire crackles and dims. Maria points an accusatory finger towards it and looks at Joanne.

"Look, the fire's dying! Even it's giving up on this shitty place!" she shouts.

"Fires die. It's a thing. And there's more wood in the mudroom, you don't have to get all melodramatic."

Maria stands up, letting her blanket slide to the floor.

"I can get it," Joanne tells her, moving to get up.

"Don't," she says, holding up a hand, "I'll get it. And I'm not being melodramatic."

Maria crosses her arms, goosebumps crawling along her skin as she walks through the dark and freezing house to the mudroom. She keeps her eyes focused on the ground as she passes the kitchen window, scared to look in case the figure's standing there. She unlocks the mudroom door, pushes it open, and walks to the pile of wood in the corner of the room. She crouches by the stack, piles a few of the small logs in her arms, and stands.

The figure is looking in the front door.

She drops the firewood and takes a step back, tripping on the bench, her eyes still glued to the thing outside.

The figure is only a few feet from the glass and he watches as she gasps in pain, her ankle turning awkwardly underneath the weight of her body as she falls to the floor. She can't help but notice that his black eyes stand out even in the swirling white all around him. He moves closer to the window and puts a hand on the glass, frost swirling out from his palm and snaking its way over the window.

Maria screams and pushes herself to her feet, limping out of the mudroom as fast as her sprained ankle will allow. She slams the door shut behind her and locks it. She turns, leaning her back against the wooden door, and screams again when she doesn't recognise the figure rushing towards her in the darkness. She closes her eyes and covers her head with her hands in panic.

"What's wrong? What happened?"

Realizing it's Joanne, Maria takes a few calming breaths before finally speaking.

"The guy from before, he's out there," she says, gesturing to the room behind her. "He was standing outside when I was getting the wood. He was watching me."

"Are you sure? 'Cause the last time you said there was someone—"

"He was there! I saw him, and I tripped, and I twisted my fucking leg!"

Joanne helps Maria to the table, where she takes a seat on one of the chairs. Once Maria's comfortable—and once Joanne's convinced she didn't accidentally break her leg—she goes back to the locked door.

"What the hell are you doing?" Maria shouts.

Maria watches in stunned silence as Joanne unlocks the door to the mudroom and pulls it open, checking to make sure no one's hiding inside or waiting by the door.

"Son of a bitch!" she shouts.

"What?" Maria screams, getting ready to run.

When Joanne doesn't answer she gets up and limps to the room, grabbing onto the counters and walls for support. She looks inside the mudroom to see Joanne struggling to shut the front door and she helps her to close it—the wind fighting them with all its might—but eventually they force the heavy door shut and bolt it in place.

"The wood's ruined," Joanne grumbles.

"Why?"

Joanne picks one of the logs up for Maria to examine; it's covered in snow, some of which has already started melting in the shelter from the wind.

"It's damp, Maria. We can't use damp wood to light a fire. Fuck! Why did you leave the door open?"

"I didn't! The man must have broken in!"

Joanne motions around the empty room.

"What man? There's no one here except for us!"

"I never said he was in here!" Maria counters, face flushed with frustration. "He was out there! He was in the snow, at the window. He was just watching me, staring at me, and he came up to the window and put his hand to the glass. Frost started coming out of his palm and, oh!" she gets excited, gesturing to the window he marked with spirals of ice, "See? Look! Frost on the inside!"

"All of the windows are covered with frost on the inside. Do you know why? Because you left the fucking door open!" Joanne yells.

"I didn't leave it open! The man did."

"There's no man!" Joanne shouts. "Look around you. Do you see any man standing here? Do you know how insane you sound talking about some mystery figure shooting frost out of his hands? Maria, I don't know what your problem is, but you have got to get a grip of yourself. There's no one out there."

Joanne walks to one of the hooks on the wall and grabs a pair of snow pants, pulling them on in a huff. She sits on the bench and tucks the thick outerwear into her boots, lacing them up tightly.

"Where are you going?" Maria asks frantic.

"To the barn. We need wood cause someone—be it you, the wind, or your mystery stalker—left the door open."

She rifles through a nearby box, taking out a scarf, a pair of warm gloves, and a balaclava that she pulls down over her thick hair.

"You can't go out during a whiteout!"

"So you want us to freeze instead?"

"We have blankets, and parkas, and——"

"It's going to get even colder than it is now, Maria. It's not even eight and I'm freezing my tits off, and you want us to go without fire for the rest of the night?"

"Joanne, there's someone out there. I saw him."

"I'll take my chances," she says, unconvinced.

Joanne pulls a parka off one of the hooks and throws it on over the rest of her outdoor clothing. She opens the door, the forces of the wind nearly blowing her backwards, and steps out into the night. She grabs the door with a gloved hand and pulls, Maria helping to close it from the other side.

"I have my keys," Joanne shouts over the storm, "so lock the door and wait for me in the living room. I'll be back soon."

"I love you!" Maria screams as the two of them finally get the door shut.

She hopes Joanne heard her.

Maria sits in front of the fireplace, blankets piled on top of the winter coat and scarf she's bundled in, embers fading to black in the dark room. She grabs another blanket from the small pile she's brought next to her and tries not to sob.

It's been hours since Joanne left and she still hasn't come back.

Deep in her bones Maria knows the figure got her. Killed her. Turned her to frost, and ice, and snow. She imagines his eyes of black watching as the life is drained from Joanne's body. Maria closes her eyes and covers her ears with her hands, imagining Joanne's scream on the winds at her door.

She sits quietly, the chattering of her teeth and the raging wind the only noises filling the ever growing silence. When she can't take the cold any longer, she reaches for another blanket from the pile, but there aren't any left. She pushes herself to her feet—pain from her ankle shooting up her leg and down deep into her foot—and makes her way to the stairwell, blankets hanging off her shoulders like a cape.

She holds onto the banister and moves slowly. She takes a step with her left leg, then moves her sore one onto the same step, making progress at a snail's pace. Eventually she gets to the top of the stairs and shuffles towards the master bedroom, socks sliding easily across the hardwood floors. She pulls the blankets off her and Joanne's queen sized bed, and drags them behind her as she makes her slow descent. She rounds the corner to the living room and freezes.

Cold black eyes are looking in through the glass doors.

Maria stares, trying to get a good look at the figure that's practically pressed against the glass, but can't. Despite only a few inches of glass separating the man from her living room, all she can see are his black eyes; the rest of him is engulfed in shadow. She stands still—petrified—as he reaches a hand to the handle of the patio door and gives a slow pull, but the door doesn't open.

"Go away," she says, voice hardly a whisper.

He grabs the handle with both hands and pulls again, but still the lock won't give way.

"Go away!" she yells, the blankets sliding to the floor around her feet.

He places a hand to the glass, frost spiraling out from the center of his palm. It swirls over the patio door, covers the handle, and coats the metal lock inside. The frost begins to thicken and harden into ice, and Maria watches as small translucent veins form along the window. The lines grow slowly and, even though she knows she should run, she remains immobile as they crawl across the glass. Only when she begins to hear a faint crackling does she realize the lines are cracks in the glass.

She feels lightheaded, the sound of blood pumping through her veins fills her ears and blocks out the noise of the glass. Her knees are weak and her legs threaten to buckle under her.

The shadow-man crumples his hand into a fist and punches it hard into the door, which breaks easily in the extreme cold. A million shards of ice and glass mix together on the wooden floor in front of Maria, a few stray pieces sliding towards her and stopping inches from her feet.

It's the jolt she needs.

She turns from the patio door and makes her way to the front entrance as the man follows Maria through her home. She runs as fast as she can which, given the state of her ankle, isn't fast at all. She throws open the door to the mudroom and slams it behind her before hurrying to the front door. She fumbles with the locks, her hands stiff from the cold, and tries not to scream in fear when she hears the mudroom door creak open behind her.

She manages to release the last of the deadbolts, and throws the front door open, the wind nearly pushing her back into the shadow figure. She rushes outside and begins to limp up the lane towards the barn. It's hard work and slow going; the wind pushes her around, thick mounds of snow cling to her jeans, and ice hiding under the drifts of white threatens to trip her. She shivers as she moves, the cold cutting bone deep and sending sharp pains shooting through her body. Her skin is cold, but knowing the shadow-man is close on her heels fills her with red hot fear.

She keeps running, legs growing tired, and Maria can't help but wonder how much farther the barn is. She should have come upon it by now, should have been able to lock herself safely inside, but she hasn't and keeps running. She can feel the man close behind her, his hands reaching for her skin, his eyes glued to her back.

Maria collides with something solid ahead of her and shouts in pain, bringing her hands to her face. Blood flows freely from her nose, the bone broken and slanted at the wrong angle. She tries to continue forward, but can't.

Something's grabbed hold of her coat.

She screams, her voice shrill and desperate, and she thrashes against the wind. She can feel the shadow-man's hands grabbing onto her, his nails of grey smoke shredding through her jacket. She spins around to face him, her parka coming free of his grip, and she tries to push him off of her. The man pushes her hard and her back collides with the solid object. She yells as he claws at her, leaving scratches down the side of her face, and he pulls her hair.

"Let me go!" she screams, voice hardly past her lips before it's carried away by the wind.

The shadow-man wraps his hands around her throat, squeezing impossibly tight. She grabs his wrists and tries to push him off. When that doesn't work, she beats her hands against his chest and pulls at his fingers around her neck, but his grip doesn't waver and she struggles to draw in air through her tight throat.

As everything begins to dim, Maria tries to make out the man's face. Even though he's only inches from her own she can only make out shadow, snow, and those eyes.

Those black eyes.

The sun had hardly pierced through the night sky when the winds finally died down and the snow was still. Joanne—huddled in a corner of the barn, covered in hay and shielded by both the front and stall doors—stares at the few stray rays making their way through the dirty windows.

There's a loud sound—the creaking of a door and loud wood being dragged through ice and heavy snow—and it jolts Joanne out of her trance.

"Maria?" she calls, voice hoarse from a night spent calling for help.

She uncurls her legs and flexes her toes, her muscles stiff, and works the kinks out of her system. When she's finally worked them all out she stands up and shuffles towards the exit of the barn, still shivering uncontrollably. Her eyes are bloodshot and she's exhausted after forcing herself to stay awake through the night in case hypothermia tried to take her while she was asleep.

She pushes the door of the barn open wider, putting her shoulder into it as she forces the heavy wood through the heaps of snow. Her body hurts and her hands and arms are sore from hours spent beating on the door, trying to force it open throughout the night.

"Maria?" she calls again, trying to figure out who's released her.

The sun blinds her as she steps out of the barn, and she blinks quickly as her vision returns. Once Joanne is able to see again, she immediately wishes she wasn't.

The bile is out of her mouth before her brain can fully process the scene in front of her. It spills over her lips and down her chin onto her parka, and she wipes her mouth with the back of a gloved hand. She looks up again, brain screaming, and braces herself against the wooden door.

A padlock that wasn't there yesterday afternoon rattles in the rusty steel latch.

Maria stands by one of the trees on the property in the opposite direction of the barn. Her body is leaning away from the trunk, her scarf caught in the snow-covered branches, arms hanging limp by her sides. Her skin is tinged blue, body and bloated face covered in flakes of white, and her throat is bruised purple.

Joanne crosses the distance between her and Maria's body, and she sinks to the ground in front of it.

Joanne wraps her arms around Maria's stiff legs and cries into the frozen denim. She realizes, as she begins to move the snow away from her wife's corpse, that Maria had run out without her boots on. No gloves, no hat, no snow pants, just her coat and the scarf Joanne knitted for her last winter.

Joanne stands and begins to unravel the scarf from the tree, trying not to look at Maria's wide and horrified eyes. She can't help but notice swirls of frost spiralling away from the tight fabric.

He was just watching me, staring at me, and he came up to the window and put his hand to the glass. Frost started coming out of his palm ...

A shiver passes down Joanne's spine. She looks around the empty fields expecting to see a man, a shadow, something, but there's no-one. Only the snow, glimmering in the rising sun.

And a pair of black eyes watching her from the woods.

THE MIDAS

"You have to turn it more," Lewis says, grabbing the metal wheel of the watertight door with both hands and pulling it to the right. There's a low click as the door closes fully, the steel bolts sliding into place. "If you don't close the compartment door all the way before opening the water hatch, you'll flood the Midas II. Try it again," he says, turning the Dog to the left until it opens.

Robat, his assistant, grabs the handle and spins it to the right once again. It closes silently, so he gives it another twist until he hears the dull click of everything locking into place.

"Good," Lewis tells him with a smile, "make sure to do it just like that when I leave."

"Will do," he says cheerfully. "Did you need me to help you gear up or—?"

"No, that won't be necessary. Just double-check the oxygen and power levels while I suit up. Oh, and if you get the chance before I do, make sure comms is up and we can get through to dispatch."

His assistant nods and turns his attention back to the display in front of him. He takes his clipboard off its resting spot atop the console and begins checking the numbers on the screen, scratching his pen against the paper in the dim light of the research submarine. He stops occasionally to look out of the large glass windows that make up most of the vessel, smiling as some unrecognizable fish swims past the glass and disappears back into the black of the ocean. Lewis is tempted to turn on the exterior lights for Robat, so he can experience the beauty and mystery of the ocean's midnight zone with his own eyes, but he doesn't want to startle the marine life before he needs to. It's bad enough he'll be walking among them with his suit on in a few short minutes.

Lewis climbs out of his chair, squeezing himself through the low door and into the release trunk of the submarine, wishing they'd made the Midas II a little bigger. The research submarine had been designed with maneuverability, resource efficiency, and tiny crews in mind. The last time he'd been on the vessel, it had been a one-man mission to observe a local pod of humpback whales. Now, he's brought his assistant to man it while he collects samples from the Bathyal zone around them, and while he's been grateful for the company and the extra set of hands, he is desperate to be back on land where he'll have personal space and elbow room.

The release trunk is just big enough to fit Lewis, the glass above him touching the tip of his hair. Once he wiggles into the pressure-resistant wetsuit and helmet, he'll have to crouch in order to fit the confined space. He pulls one leg on and then the other, stopping to make sure the attached flippers are well secured around his feet, before pulling his arms into the suit. The reflective material gleams in his hand, and he's excited to wear it in the water. He buckles the chest closed and double checks all the zippers and clasps, thankful that these new suits can be done up without assistance. He remembers the older atmospheric diving suits from the display in the university museum and shudders at the thought of wearing such a bulky and restrictive device underwater. Although his wetsuit is tethered to the submarine for oxygen and power, its modern design allows for increased mobility and ease of wear while still keeping safe from the pressure of the ocean.

"How's it going?" Robat asks, turning away from the dashboard and looking at Lewis in the small chamber.

"Finished, I think! Can you perform the safety check, please?"

Robat nods and approaches the small compartment, squeezing into the uncomfortably small space with his mentor. He double-checks the clasps and zippers before making sure the watertight cable that both powers the suit and keeps the oxygen flowing to the diver is connected securely.

Robat pats his thighs, a job well done, and makes his way back into the main chamber of the Midas II, careful not to rub against Lewis and accidentally unlatch anything from the suit as he passes by in the tight space. He checks the levels on the dash one more time before radioing their current position to the team ashore.

"Midas II, this is Gavin Evans from control. Your position has been noted and you can begin deployment when ready, over."

"Noted. Thanks. Over and out," Robat says, letting go of the push-to-talk button on the handheld device and placing it back on the dash.

"Ready when you are," Lewis says excitedly.

Robat gives him a thumbs up before closing the door to the compartment, turning the metal wheel as far as it will go, and pressing the large black button on the control panel. With a loud thud, the back panel of the submarine opens and water begins to force its way into the small compartment. The door opens wider and wider, metal gears spinning and clicking into place as the door gives way to the black of the ocean.

Lewis pushes himself out of the compartment, kicking his legs and propelling himself forward into the dark. The cable unfurls behind him as he moves through the water, stopping once he's a few feet out.

"Lewis, this is Robat," his assistant says through the speaker in his helmet. "I'm ready to begin illumination on your mark, over."

"Robat, this is Lewis," he says, pressing the side of his helmet and activating the comms mic inside. "Illuminate at will. Over and out."

There's a soft click as Robat hangs up and Lewis holds his breath, waiting silently in the dark.

And then he sees it.

At first, it looks like stars dancing along his suit, specks shimmering in the black as the strings of high-powered lights woven into the waterproof material spring to life and paint the ocean around him with bright light.

It's like magic, he thinks in awe as the ocean floor drips with gold.

Lewis' wetsuit is the crowning achievement of his career. It is a wetsuit designed not just for mobility, but for visibility. The bright lights illuminate the water and the reflective nature of the material engulfs the wearer in a halo of amber light. It makes deep-sea rescues easier for crews, makes exploration and sample collection a one-person job, and can light up the murky waters of the midnight zone like no hand-held lamp that has come before it. He named the suit the Midas for the golden glow it bathes the world in, and the small fleet of submarines—all equipped with Lewis' wetsuit—have each taken the name in turn.

The ocean floor has always been beautiful even without the help of Lewis or his suit, but with the golden tint illuminating the blackened waters, the ocean is unrecognizable. The fish and sea creatures move around him, ripples of yellows and oranges cutting kaleidoscopic patterns through the water. The sand shimmers and pulsates in the light emanating from his body, the tiny rocks of beige and brown transforming into specks of precious metals that swirl as fish rush by in surprise at the sudden glow. Something skitters by him in the sand, a dull crab now decorated as some ethereal and otherworldly being.

Lewis moves through the water, swimming further and further away from the oppressive walls of the Midas II. He knows that the submarine doesn't have enough oxygen for him to dally too long, not if he wants to collect all the samples he's been sent out to collect, but he can't stop himself from stealing a few precious minutes to forget his obligations and enjoy the calmness that the ocean brings. Down here, wrapped in the golden glow of the lights, he is just another creature drifting aimlessly through the cold water.

Then, just as suddenly as the lights came on, they shut back off.

"Robat, this is Lewis from the Midas. We've lost power to the lights. What seems to be the problem? Over."

Silence.

"Robat, what's going on? Over."

He waits, his call left unanswered.

"Robat, come in, over."

When Robat doesn't answer, Lewis' heart sinks and his lungs feel too tight. The Midas is still feeding him oxygen, but Lewis swears he suddenly can't breathe. It's dark in the water once more. Here, deep in the midnight zone, he can't see his hand in front of his face. He takes hold of the cable connecting him to the Midas II and follows it back to the submarine, gathering it in loops wound around his hand and kicking his legs through the heavy liquid, muscles stiff from the long hours in the ship now made sore from the frantic swimming.

He knows something is horribly wrong before he sees the Midas II or, more accurately, when he *doesn't* see the Midas II. The faint waspy-yellow lights of the control panel should have been visible through the glass window. But now the Midas II is as black as the waters around it as it rests against the ocean floor.

Lewis propels himself forward and reaches a hand out, letting his gloved fingers run along the outer glass wall of the Midas II as he blindly moves through the ocean, trying to figure out what's happened. He locates the door to the release trunk, opens it, and moves slowly inside the ship. He clings to the wall and feels his way along with his hands, taking care not to swim headfirst into a wall or snag himself on something sharp. The water-tight door is open before Lewis gets there and he realizes with horror that Robat didn't close it right after he left the ship.

Something heavy moves against his leg in the hull of the vessel and when he reaches out to feel it, his fingers brush against someone else's hand.

It's Robat's hand.

Lewis feels sick, bile creeping up the back of his throat, but he forces himself to swallow it down. If he's sick in the suit it could clog the opening of the cables still supplying him with oxygen and then he'd find himself like his assistant. He breathes deep, in through the nose and out through his mouth, trying to steady his nerves. Eventually, the nausea passes and he's able to talk without wanting to throw up. He presses the side of his helmet, the communication mic crackling to life.

"This is Lewis from the Midas, does anyone read me? Over."

He waits.

"This is Lewis from the Midas, does anyone in control read me? Over."

There's a low pop and a fizzle as the line comes to life.

"This is Gavin Evans from control. We read you, Lewis. Over."

A sob he didn't know he was holding in escapes him, relieved to hear a voice on the other end of the line. The comfort of knowing he's not alone washes over him before turning into guilt as he's reminded that Robat had no one in his final moments.

"The Midas II has sunk. Robat is dead. I'm still tethered to the ship and have oxygen, but my main power is out and I don't know how much air I have left. I need an emergency evacuation ship sent out immediately. Over."

The mic on the other end is silent and Lewis' heart beats fast during the long pause.

"Lewis," Gavin's voice finally says, "we Roger your distress call. The Midas IV has been notified of your last known location and is being dispatched for your recovery. Over."

"And Robat. They need to get Robat." As an afterthought, he adds, "Over."

"The Midas IV is being re-routed to your location and will be at capacity once you've boarded. The Midas III has also been alerted of your distress call and will be dispatched upon your recovery. Please be sure to stay in a visible location close to your vessel. We ask that you also keep the comms channel open and conserve power. We're coming to get you, Lewis. Over and out."

Gavin's microphone fades to static before dissolving into silence. Lewis floats in the blackened waters that fill the hull of the Midas II, Robat's lifeless body pressed against him. A fresh wave of grief washes over him as he pictures the young man—so full of energy and excitement at being called to work alongside Lewis—bloated and blue, eyes bulging and mouth open, his tongue lolling out. Robat's body bumps into him again and it sends a shiver through Lewis. He pushes his assistant's corpse away from him before making his way back through the water-tight door, out the door of the release trunk, and back into the open water. He closes the outer door to the Midas II, not wanting Robat to float away into the sea, or for some creature to wander into the ship looking for food, and he waits.

Things move through the water around him. A fish swims so close to the glass of his helmet that he can almost count the gills on the small animal despite the darkness of the Bathyal zone. A crab—he thinks it's a crab—scuttles over his foot, the toe of his flipper sticking into the sand and anchoring him in place. He feels something move along his arm and he can't help but panic and shake it off, likely spooking a bottom feeder searching for food. But in his mind, alone in the black, he can't help but imagine it's a gulper eel trying to rip into his suit to devour him.

He closes his eyes, trying not to imagine the forms moving around him, their predatory bodies carving ripples of black in the murky grey water. Instead, he thinks of the honey-gold light of the Midas banishing the shadows and transforming the ocean into a masterpiece that could have been painted by Klimt himself. He thinks about the rows of light, flickering to life then burning bright like a wildfire, and how they dance along the metallic surface of the Midas and transform him from a man into the very sun itself.

But when Lewis opens his eyes, he's not shining bright like a celestial being.

He's alone in the dark.

He's not sure how much time has passed since he closed his eyes, but in the silence and stillness of the water, it feels like he's spent a lifetime down here. He tries to keep his breathing even and steady, not wanting to deplete his oxygen faster than he needs to. He stares into the distant water, watching as the black fades to slate, then to Oxford blue, then to—

His heart beats violently against his bones, sending tremors up his spine, as he watches the water grow brighter in the distance. At first, he thinks it's a trick of his mind, the isolation and desperation making him imagine people in the distance, but soon a ray of yellow cuts the black and he knows he's safe. He sobs with relief, allowing himself to cry for his own salvation and for the death of Robat, before attempting to pull himself together before the rescue crew gets to him.

He presses the button on the side of his helmet, waiting patiently as the mic pops to life.

"Control, this is Lewis of the Midas, do you read me? Over."

"Lewis, this is Gavin from control. Over."

"I can see the light from the Midas IV approaching. They're on course to find the vessel. Over."

"I'll relay the information to the crew. Please keep the channel open and communicate any change in their visibility. Over and out," Gavin says, his microphone going offline with a click.

Even though the suit is waterproof, Lewis' body is slicked wet and damp with sweat. His limbs hurt from trying to keep himself anchored to the sunken submarine, and he's exhausted from the panic and anguish that have been trapped inside him since the lights of the Midas went out.

The glow in the distance grows closer, the faint illumination turning from a light dandelion to the washed-out colour of a yellow jacket and then into a deep shade of mustard. The light grows as it gets closer, and soon it looks like a carpet of aureolin is being rolled out on the ocean floor exclusively for Lewis. The reflective surface of the Midas picks up the approaching light and casts it around him in a halo. Even though his oxygen must be running low, he feels like he can breathe for the first time since being stranded in the water.

The light moves slowly towards him, getting stronger as it advances, and Lewis begins to wave his arms back and forth in the water, trying to move them fast despite the resistance. He bends his torso to the left and to the right as he waves his arms, trying to catch and reflect as much of the gold as his suit can. As if in response to his gestures, the light moves faster towards him.

In the distance, a second light emerges out of the black. It's faint and made of amber and begins following the pattern of the first light, tracing its way along the ocean floor towards him. It moves at a much slower pace than the orb fast approaching him, and he wonders if the crew has lost his location.

Lewis presses the side of his helmet, the microphone popping to life.

"This is Lewis of the Midas. I see the Midas IV headed directly for me and I can see the Midas VI in the distance confirming that they're on course to my location. Over."

The mustard light gets closer, bouncing off the suit of the Midas and beginning to reflect off the glass walls of the sunken observation ship resting on the sand. As it approaches him the rays get brighter, blindingly so, but Lewis still can't make out the submarine it's originating from. He squints and shields his eyes through his helmet with a gloved hand, worried that the vessel is getting too close.

"Lewis, this is Gavin from control. Midas VI hasn't been dispatched. They're awaiting your recovery. The crew of the Midas IV are struggling to get a visual on you. They're beginning pulsations. Can you confirm you see them? Over."

In the distance, the light fades to black then gold. Black. Gold.

The light rushes closer and in its neon glow Lewis makes out more than just gold; he sees white and rust and red and black. Yellow eyes stare through him into the depths of the water, watching him with predatory precision from behind a glowing lure at the end of a dorsal rod.

The anglerfish closes its mouth around Lewis's midsection before he even knows to scream, its razor-sharp teeth cutting through the safety of the Midas and deep into the man's flesh. They're like hot knives through butter, and they trap him in the fish's jaw as it continues to swim through the black, pulling Lewis away from the safety of the Midas II. Water begins to rush in through the tears in his suit, and if the sudden pressure from the midnight zone hadn't already crushed Lewis' lungs he'd be screaming.

"This is Gavin from control. Can you confirm you see the pulsa—"

The comms go quiet as the cable tethering Lewis to the ship is disconnected, the beast dragging his body well past the cord's limit. As Lewis bleeds out in the water, he watches his blood cloud the yellow light of the anglerfish and paint the ocean gold.

HUNGER

Originally Published in Sanitarium Magazine *Issue No. 23*

Snow blankets the forest floor. Every rock covered by a thick duvet of white, each bush stripped of green. Strong winds beat against the walls of the log cabin, rattling the icicles like wind chimes. It hisses through the cracks in the window and chills the two men inside, and even the orange glow of the morning light can't warm them.

"There hasn't been a hint of life for weeks, Jean. Probably longer."

"Then they're bound to be here soon, right? Everything happens when you least expect it," the man replies through chattering teeth, "so help's bound to knock on the door any minute."

"Yeah... or death is," Pierre says quietly.

"Shut up. You keep thinking like that and one day you'll wake up dead. Stay p-p-p-p-positive."

Pierre glares at Jean, but doesn't press on; his lips crack and bleed every time he speaks. Cold claws at his throat each time he opens his mouth. He can hardly feel his hands, and hasn't been able to feel his toes for days. At first they hurt when he walked, but the pain has faded and been replaced by a lack of feeling entirely. He wants to make sure they haven't gone black, but he's afraid to expose them any more to the harsh winter than they've already been. His bones hurt from the ice he's convinced has begun to grow on them, but worse is the pain in his stomach.

Neither he nor Jean have eaten proper food for longer than he thinks possible. He feels thinner and is sure he's lost weight. Staring at Jean, he wonders if he looks anything like his nephew now does. With his sunken eyes, hollow cheeks, and thinning frame, Jean looks like a shadow of himself.

Game has been impossible to find since the storm hit. What few plants they found made them sick, and the bark they've torn from the trees is hard to eat and gives them little in sustenance. They ran out of water within the first week, and out of matches and dry lumber a week after that. Reduced to eating the snow to keep hydrated, along with whatever germs cling to it, Pierre can't help but think the ever-throbbing pain in his chest isn't entirely caused by starvation.

"That's it," Pierre says, in a frail voice. "We need to get out. And we need to go now."

"I'm not going anywhere. We just need to be patient, just a little longer, and then we'll—"

"—die a slow death, trapped in a cabin."

Jean pulls a pine needle from inside his coat pocket and slowly begins to gnaw on it.

"It's better than dying lost in a forest, or being eaten by starving wolves."

"I'd welcome the wolves, Jean. At least then I'd have a chance to bite some meat off one of them, and die with a full stomach. Besides, the dogs had enough brains to get out of here a long while ago."

"There's still some. How else do you account for the howling outside our cabin all night?"

"The wind," he shoots back, dismissively.

"Or a demon," Jean says quietly, in a whisper.

"Demons?"

"Demons. Mom used to tell me stories of how your father's ancestors lived in these woods and how the forest was plagued with them. She said to me that her—your—great grandfather was almost tricked into becoming one, but he saved himself in time."

"My grandfather—"

"Your great grandfather—"

"Was almost a demon?" Pierre laughs bitterly.

"It's true! Mom told me that when he was a young boy he was tracking a moose with some men from town, when he and his friend got separated from them. The moose led them all through the woods, for many days, until both of them were lost and hungry. The moose tracks had disappeared days before and there wasn't any game to hunt. They grew so hungry, that one day an evil spirit overcame him. Mom told me he was possessed by the urge to eat his frie—"

"I've had enough of you and your fucking demons. I'm sick of you blaming every twig snap, gust of air, or wild animal on them. They're not real. They never were real."

Pierre pulls his blanket closer to him. Despite the fire from his words, he's shivering. His teeth chatter so hard that he worries they'll begin to chip. He glares at Jean, who continues to silently chew his pine needle. His brow's furrowed together and, like Pierre, he shakes with cold. His lips crack as he works to finish the only food he has.

Pierre looks away from his young nephew and out the window. He feels bad for being harsh with him, but the forest is frightening enough without him adding monsters to it. Demons and evil forces are nothing to worry about, not while winter hardship is at their door. Pierre's grandfather hadn't been told by a monster to eat his friend; he was driven by the human need to survive. He'd been desperate, not possessed.

"We should leave now, while there's enough daylight to," Pierre suggests.

"I told you, I don't want to go."

"I wasn't asking if you wanted to do it. I was telling you what we're going to do."

Jean swallows the last of his pine needle and coughs hard. "I said no. Yves tried to find the way back to the main road and he never came back. Francois left to try and find Yves and he also never came back. There's something out there, I don't care what you say. Doesn't matter if it's a wolf, or a demon, or a big hole in the earth sucking everyone one up. There's something out there and I don't want to die. The whiteout is making it impossible to find anything! And you want us to not just find the dirt road we took to get here, but tell it apart from the other ones? Yves was the one who brought us here, and he was the only one who knew how to get back!"

They stare at each other, until Jean's eyes dart nervously away and focus on the rising sun outside. The light, slowly finding its way into the room, begins to brighten the corner where they huddle together. Jean's skin, illuminated by the sun, looks sallow. His blue eyes look dead and dark, while the deep wrinkles carved into his skin make him look years older. Although he's young enough to hardly be a man, he looks old enough to be a father.

Looking at him, Pierre's filled with regret at letting Jean come hunting with them. He'd never fired a gun in his life and hadn't spent enough time in the wild to know how to be unafraid of it. Still, Pierre had hoped this trip would make him less anxious in the forest, possibly even encourage a liking for the great outdoors. Pierre had always taken it upon himself to try and keep an eye on him after Jean's father had walked out on him as a boy. Pierre had wanted to inspire a love of nature in Jean. He'd figured a trip to Yves' hunting cabin would do the trick. Now he's sure that if the two of them make it home alive, Jean will spend the rest of his life within the town borders.

But it's a very big 'if'.

"If you stay here, you'll never see home again. I promise you that. If we stay here, someone will find us. But it won't be until they're sure the whiteout's over, and probably weeks after that. And do you know what they'll find? Two men, huddling in a corner, their bodies thin and broken with their mouths hanging open. They'll find two men who spent their last moments begging for food, or water, or death."

Jean closes his eyes, and rests his head against his bent knees. He trembles with fear, both at the idea of leaving and that of staying.

"We don't even have water, Jean. We're eating dirty snow, and getting sick from it. I know you can feel it too. So if we don't die of starvation, it'll be from something we ate trying to keep from dying of thirst. And if it isn't that, then it'll be the cold."

Jean sniffles, his frail body quivering. His muffled crying slowly fades to silence. Jean wipes his eyes, though the tears have already frozen to his face.

"Ok," he says, quietly, "but if we find nothing by late afternoon, we come back here. I don't want to be out in the night, when there's nothing but the stars to light up the woods."

Pierre nods in agreement, and begins to stretch out his limbs. He rubs his muscles awake, and tries to ignore the screams of protest from his stiff joints. He can't feel his feet, and his legs hardly support his weight. He wants to fall back onto the floor, but survival keeps him standing. Jean's even slower to his feet than Pierre, and rocks unsteadily once he's finally up. Jean leans against the cabin wall, legs shaking, and Pierre wonders if making Jean leave is the right choice. Perhaps his reluctance to go hasn't been entirely out of fear, but from his inability to walk.

Pierre wraps his blanket tightly around himself, making sure it covers as much of him as it can, and holds the loose ends close to his chest. His fingers tingle, erasing any doubt about leaving: tingling was the first thing his toes did before all sensation left them. He's sure the skin's dead or dying, and has no intention of losing his fingers too. He opens the door to the wooden cabin and snow hurls itself inside the room, coating the floor in white. While Jean shuffles his way to the door, Pierre begins to fight his way through the snow.

The forest floor is a sea of white that reaches to his knees and sucks out what little warmth his legs have. Each step's laborious, slow, and tells him to go back. Except he can't go back, not when his stomach's so empty it threatens to eat itself. Not when he's so cold his heart pumps slush through his veins instead of blood. Pierre forces himself to clear a path through the snow, ploughing a trail for Jean to follow. It's slow work, and takes them a long while to get past their hatchback.

The truck's coated in a thick layer of ice, the chipped red paint hardly showing through. The gas line froze the first night of the storm, leaving the car a useless piece of metal. They'd torn the car apart after the first week, stripping it of anything that could be useful. They'd used what gas they could extract to keep their fires from dying, but it hadn't been enough. The interior had been stripped of any leather they could find, which they'd boiled to eat. When the dyes in the upholstery had begun to make them sick, they'd wrapped themselves in the leather scraps to keep warm. Yves had left with the last of them.

Although he can't see into the truck, he knows there's a bright yellow tennis ball that belonged to his hound still in the backseat. He feels a stab of regret; after the last of the food, and with no signs of game to hunt, Pierre's dog had been the next thing to go. He hadn't wanted to do it. He'd wanted to wait for Francois and Yves to come back, but it had been so long since they'd left. Even though he'd raised that dog since it had been a pup, Jean had been so weak and hungry, and Pierre had vowed to watch over him. He'd held his dog quietly through the night, and come sunrise he snapped its neck. He made sure they'd used everything. The fur, the meat—they'd even boiled the bones more times than they'd been good for. The only thing left of his dog was a pile of gnawed-on bones, and the bright yellow tennis ball.

As Pierre forces himself onward, he comes to a tree that has been badly damaged by the storm. Its branches, weighed down by the ice and snow, have broken off and fallen uselessly around it. Its furthest branches, blown off by the wind, lie on the ground like useless limbs. He turns back towards Jean to warn him to watch his footing once past the truck, only to find his nephew much farther behind him than ex-pected.

Jean takes slow and small steps, trying to walk where the snow's already cleared, but too weak to manage the same large steps as Pierre. His lips are bleeding sluggishly from the small cracks, and the skin on his face is chapped red. Pierre picks up two of the longer branches and makes his way back to Jean.

"Thanks," Jean says, but his words are rushed away by the wind before they can be heard. He leans on the branch, with one hand on the back of Pierre's shoulder for additional support, and they continue into the woods.

By late morning a thick coat of snow has gathered on their blankets, freezing the thick wool stiff and solid. They move at half the speed they left at, making remarkably little progress along where they imag-ine the road to be and into the forest. Although the cabin's out of sight, they can feel it in the distance, watching them carve a path to where they hope to find safety and warmth. From somewhere in the depths of the land comes a low and long howl.

"There it is again," Jean says, weakly. "It's following us. It knows I'm going to die, doesn't it?" he asks, voice thick with panic.

The wind came to a stop a while ago, but flakes of ivory continue to fall lazily. Jean's arm is slung across Pierre's shoulders, leaning heavily on his uncle to help keep him standing. With his other hand he clings to the branch, putting some of his weight on that to help lighten Pierre's load. Jean's lips are tinged blue and his stomach aches.

"You're not g-g-g-going to die," Pierre tells him.

"Why is it following us?"

"Maybe it's not following us. Maybe it's leading us to the road," Pierre says encouragingly, "or to food! I've heard stories of wolves, or stray dogs that help lead people to safety in times of need."

"You said all the wolves were gone."

"I guess I was wrong."

"Or it's not a wolf."

As if on cue, another howl cuts through the air. It's louder this time and much closer. Jean begins to shake hard, from cold and from fear, and walks with more urgency. They come to the edge of a snow hill and, deciding that they will spend as much effort going over it as they would going around it, begin to climb. Trusting Jean to keep himself standing for a minute, Pierre begins pushing the snow to the side with his hands, uncovering dark red stains beneath the surface in the process.

"What is that?" Jean asks, already knowing the answer.

"Blood. Maybe there's a dead rabbit, or fox, maybe even a doe, under here that we can eat," Pierre says excitedly.

He pulls fistfuls of snow off the mound, hoping that what's underneath will be worth this time and effort. It seems large, but not big enough that it can be a deer. His mind feels foggy, his appetite urging him to dig deeper. As he moves another pile of white to the side, he's rewarded with a tuft of dark brown hair. A second heave reveals more brown hair. A third reveals a pale blue forehead. A fifth and he's face to face with the dead body of Yves.

His friend's eyes are wide with terror, mouth agape in a frozen scream. The left side of his face is torn to shreds, muscle and flayed tissue hanging off bone. A pool of blood that has collected in his open mouth, and that coats his skin, is frozen solid.

Behind him comes the dull thud of Jean falling to the ground, followed by the sound of stomach acid being heaved into the snow. The acrid stench of bile cuts the air as another howl calls out.

"Leave us alone!" shouts Jean.

Pierre continues to stare into the eyes of his friend, his reflection shown back to him in the frozen blood gathered on Yves. His full, fat, meaty cheek, hardly touched by famine. Pierre can't help but think that if his face still looks full, then the rest of him is sure to still be carrying some meat. Unless whatever's torn off part of his face has taken other parts with it. Except Yves had been missing for weeks and he's frozen to the core, so Pierre's sure that whatever's left will be impossible to—

He stops his brain before it can finish that thought. His heart beats loud as the realization of what he's considered sinks in. How calculated he's been, trying to figure out what can be used, what can be rationed. Although he tells himself those thoughts are just his way of coping with the discovery of his deceased friend, the growling in his stomach and the spit coating his tongue say otherwise.

"We need to go," says Pierre quickly.

"We need to go back," shoots Jean.

"We can't go back now! Do you know how long it took us to get here? There is no going back," he yells, helping Jean to his unsteady feet. "We keep going forward."

Jean nods slowly, his whole body trembling with fear, but his eyes full of determination. Together the two of them make a path around the body of their friend and towards where they pray the main road will await them.

But by late afternoon Jean begs Pierre for them to take a break, and he reluctantly gives in. They take their rest against the trunk of a maple, its wide trunk helping to shield them from the wind that begins to pick up. When Pierre suggests they resume their course, Jean's unable to support his own weight. He can't lift himself onto his feet, and once Pierre gets him up, his legs buckle underneath him. His breathing's slow and ragged, teeth chattering hard together. His lips have gone from pale blue to a much darker shade, and his eyes look wild and empty. As Pierre encourages Jean to fight, a howl in the distance is carried to them on the wind.

"Don't let it get me," coughs Jean, his voice frail and ragged.

"I won't, but we have to keep moving."

"Promise you won't let the monster get to me," he begs.

"What?"

"The demon! Don't let it get me, Pierre. Don't let it get me, please."

"I won't," he promises.

Jean grabs his hand tight, his thin body shaking under thick clothing and a thinning sheet. He coughs, trying to catch his breath. "Don't let it get you, either," he whispers quietly.

"Never."

Jean nods and leans back against the tree, closing his eyes. Pierre watches as his nephew's chest softly rises then falls, each breath getting slower. Pierre's still holding his hand when Jean's chest falls for the last time. He sits waiting for the small intake of air that will never come. He looks at his face, the thin and patchy beard of a boy trying to be a man, the soft skin of someone too young. How childlike his face is in death. He looks like he could be sleeping, his chin resting softly against his chest with his lips parted slightly. He's a portrait of innocence dead in the snow.

Pierre's breath catches in his chest, and his throat feels too tight. His body's tired, and wants to lie down beside Jean and drift away into the winter frost with him. Except he can't. The howling is too loud and too close. The expanse of forest around him is bare of pine trees, and even though he can hear the relentless howls, he can't see the animal making them. Although he wishes Jean were alive, the thought that he's escaped is a comfort.

Pierre's eyes water, and he pulls Jean's body closer to him. It's an empty shell now, he knows that, but he wants to hold onto what little of him there is left. He's failed him, let him die deep in the woods. His mother will have no one now, no one except for Pierre, and he doesn't see how she'll ever be able to look at him again. How can his sister ever see him as anyone other than the man who let her child die? How can Pierre ever face his own children now, knowing that if it had been one of them that had come along with him, they'd be dead in his place?

Pierre will be dead soon too. He knows it, he can feel it. Jean shouldn't have worried about a monster getting him; not when nature would. Jean would have wanted him to find a way to survive, to find some way to keep going, but exhaustion sunk its claws into Pierre long ago. He wants to give up.

Pierre stares at Jean's emaciated body. It's half the size it was when they left town, but there's still some meat clinging to bone. He may have been cold from the snow, but he's not yet frozen through.

Pierre can feel saliva creeping back into his mouth as he slowly slides the blanket off his friend. He quivers as his body compels him forward, animal instincts egging him on, his brain begging him to stop. Picking up one of Jean's arms, he rolls back the sleeve and examines it, pleased to see there's more than just skin and bone. Jean would have wanted this. Jean would've wanted him to go home, to be a father to his children. Jean's death means Pierre's survival. His whole body shakes with anticipation as he brings Jean's arm close to his mouth, closes his eyes, and sinks his teeth deep into unfeeling skin. Blood trickles into his mouth, and Jean's final words hang in the air.

Don't let it get you, either.

His eyes shoot open, and he lets go of the arm. He spits out the chunk of flesh, and quickly rinses his mouth with a handful of snow. He swirls it in his mouth, letting it melt over his palette, before spitting the remaining blood out.

"Never," he tells the woods. He lifts himself from his spot on the ground, covering Jean's body with his own blanket on the way up. Without looking back, Pierre continues to force his way through the snow and ice.

By nightfall he feels battered and bruised, but as lost as ever. Jean had been right to suggest they wait for help to find them. He can feel something watching him, waiting for him to die so it can sink its teeth into him. Jean was right about it all. With each second the sun falls, so does the temperature. Pierre can feel his body shutting down. His breathing is hard, each exhale long and strained, each inhale short and sharp. His heart beats faster than it ever has, and he can feel the blood moving under his flesh with each pump. As he pushes through the snow heaps, he prepares himself for death. He braces himself for his vision to slowly turn to black, sound to be suddenly muffled and his light extinguished from the world.

As the forest grows darker, Pierre notices a small ball of light flickering in the distance. A sound somewhere between a whimper and a whoop escapes him, and he finds his legs moving quicker now that survival's more than a distant dream; it's a flame calling him home. He pushes his way through the snow, branches cutting his face as he forces his way between the saplings and into a clearing.

There's no fire. The rays of the sun, as it tucks itself away for the night, bounce off the small snow hills in the empty expanse of land. The reflection of the sun glimmers on the snow, giving an illusion of fire. Pierre stares at winter's mirage and is filled with a hopelessness that seems endless. His body hurts, and he's tired of fighting. He sinks to his knees and stares into the clearing, his eyes focused on a spot on one of the snow mounds that bounces the light back at him. Dragging himself to his feet, he wades through the thick white cover on the forest floor. With each step the ground crunches underneath him.

A small sliver of metal peeks up from the mound, and he dusts off more snow revealing a butane lighter. He huffs in excitement as he flicks it, praying for a spark. After several tries it ignites, and he silently cheers at the small stream of heat coming from the tip. He scans the forest for the owner of the flame, knowing that they couldn't have passed by here more than an hour ago. He searches for footprints, or signs of nature disturbed, but finds nothing but trees and more snow hills crowded together.

Snow hills.

Like the one Yves was buried in.

Directly behind him, a small howl pierces through the thick silence. Pierre turns around, slow on his feet, his mind shutting itself off from the world. He sees its pale blue skin, bloated stomach, elongated fingers and what looks like a human face being stretched and contorted by a wolf's skull. Its snout is long and lined with sharp teeth, framed by torn human lips pulled wider than nature should ever have allowed possible. Crossing the distance between them, it stops inches from

Pierre. It's so close that its breath, rank with the stench of meat, ruffles his hair.

The demon's smile is so much like Francois'. Pierre falls backwards into the snow, screaming. The creature moves closer, watching him curiously. He doesn't seem to understand Pierre's fright, and bends his face close to Pierre's. The beast reaches out a clawed hand towards him, and Pierre acts before he can think. He swings his branch against the monster's temple, sending it crashing to the ground. Pierre throws himself on top of the creature, finding strength in the terror. The demon screams as it thrashes beneath him. Pierre raises his branch high above his head, and the beast watches with wide eyes as he brings it down hard on his skull, again and again. There's a sickening crack.

Pierre's face is splattered in thick, red blood. He breathes heavily, and his muscles hurt from the fight. He watches as the blood trickles from the broken body into the snow around him. There's movement in the distance, as something pushes its way out of the forest across from him. Another one.

Another monster coming to kill him. It's holding a flashlight in one of its clawed hands. This beast isn't as big as the last one, or as quick. It moves towards Pierre hesitantly, then screams. It must be calling for more of them to come. He doesn't think, he doesn't have time to. He runs towards the monster, chases it through the woods. His legs threaten to buckle underneath him with every step, but he needs to catch the demon. He needs to kill it for Yves, left dead in the ice, and for Jean, who died scared, under a tree.

He catches up to the monster, and throws himself at it. They fall hard to the ground, and Pierre pins the creature under him. It screams, panicked now. Its wide eyes stare at Pierre, horrified. It thrashes underneath him, trying to buck him off, but he stays on. He won't let this monster stop him.

"This is for Jean," he hisses.

"Jean! What have you done to Jean? Pierre, what have you done? Jean!" the beast screams, in his sister's voice.

He grips the monster's throat tightly, squeezing the life out of it. It claws at his hands, trying to throw him off. He squeezes harder, watching the creature's eyes roll back in its head. He stays on top of her, panting, his hand locked around her throat for what feels like an eternity. He stays like that until the other monsters come looking.

He can hear noises and voices coming from the forest, along the path he's been following for so long. They talk loudly, calling for someone. Stray rays of light cut through the trees as they search for their dead friends.

Pierre smiles to himself and runs to face them, howling into the night.

Acknowledgements

Of all the things I've written in this collection, these acknowledgements have been the hardest to pen by far. And it's not because I can't think of anyone to thank, but because there are so many people: family members, friends, peers, teachers, editors, and *you*. Because without readers like you supporting indie horror and encouraging new voices, so many of us authors wouldn't be where we are today.

And that's a fact.

I'd be remiss if I didn't start this out by thanking my family for their years of support. They were my first test audience, beta readers, and editors. My grandfather is the one who instilled the love of storytelling in me. My mom sat through story after gruesome story, always giving me feedback when it was needed. My dad would (and still does!) collect every book, every magazine, and every scrap of paper that I'd worked on. And my brother was the one who pushed me to keep writing when I felt like giving up and doing something, *anything*, else with my life because I worried my stories would never be good enough.

I also can't forget the incredible friends who've kept me going and encouraged me along the way, like Sabrina and Lambert to name a few. I also have to give the biggest shoutout and thank you to Georgia, who I'm *convinced* is single-handedly responsible for me getting first published all those years ago and why I continue to get published today.

This book, this dream, would also not have been possible without the guidance, encouragement, and help of so many incredible people in the horror writing community. A huge thank you goes out to Barry Skelhorn, who published my first horror story; Mark Nixon, who changed my life with *Shadows at the Door*; David Tocher, who believed in my writing when I didn't; Trevor Ferguson, who was more influential on my career than he'll ever know. And of course, the biggest thank you has to go out to Antonia Ward for taking a chance on me, making me a better writer, and for bringing *Palimpsest* to life. I don't think I can put into words how much getting to work with *Ghost Orchid Press* has meant to me.

Lastly, to Tommy. I hope you know how much your love and support have meant to me. I love you (and our cats!) so *so* much. (And, *fine*, for your help with *Laughlin Hills*. You were right.)

Caitlin Marceau
2022

ABOUT THE AUTHOR

Caitlin Marceau is an author and lecturer living and working in Montreal. She holds a B.A. in Creative Writing, is a member of both the Horror Writers Association and the Quebec Writer's Federation, and spends most of her time writing horror and experimental fiction.

She's been published for journalism and poetry, as well as creative non-fiction, and has spoken about horror literature at several Canadian conventions. Her collection, *A Blackness Absolute*, is slated for publication by D&T Publishing LLC in 2022.

If she's not covered in ink or wading through stacks of paper, you can find her ranting about issues in pop culture or nerding out over a good book. For more, check out CaitlinMarceau.ca.

Also Available from Ghost Orchid Press

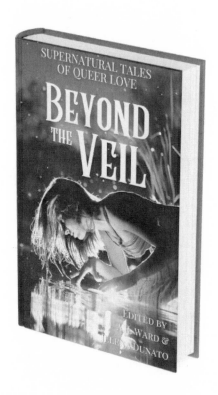

Made in United States
North Haven, CT
13 March 2022

17062923R00136